SIX MOONS

SIX MOONS

DAVID·R·FOX

BROWN
DOG
BOOKS

First published 2019

Published under licence by Brown Dog Books and
The Self-Publishing Partnership, 7 Green Park Station,
Bath BA1 1JB

www.selfpublishingpartnership.co.uk

ISBN printed book: 978-1-83952-027-3
ISBN e-book: 978-1-83952-029-7

Cover design by Mark Thomas
Internal design by Andrew Easton

Printed and bound by CPI Group (UK) Ltd, Croydon, CR0 4YY

This book is printed on FSC certified paper

MIX
Paper from
responsible sources
FSC® C013604
FSC
www.fsc.org

For Hannah

One knave, one monk whom walls surround
Their destinies together wound
Two books, wherein the answer's found
One burning brightly
The other tightly bound

1
OCTOBER

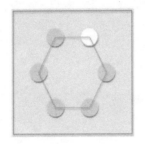

As only the very enlightened will testify, it is seldom wise to announce the rare condition of unbridled joy to the wider world. A surfeit of happiness in a person is apt to make others nervous, suspicious, inclined to morbid self-absorption. What, they wonder, is there to be so happy about? What have I missed? Whatever it is, they go on to assure themselves, it is just like me to have missed it.

Happiness can be the cause of much unhappiness.

And after all, Dromo was being punished, was he not? What right did he have to be happy, imprisoned as he was in the high tower of a castle? He lived on a diet of stale bread and thin gruel, and slept on a straw mattress in a circular cell no bigger than a dozen foot lengths from one side to the other. The stone slabs at his back froze during the winter months and sweated in the summer heat. Above him a cross-hatch of wooden beams supporting the conical roof at the very apex of the tower, the highest point of the castle, was variously home to pigeons and doves whose defecation regularly bespattered his threadbare monk's habit. And for hour upon hour there was not a soul to share his confinement with, nor mark the long day's passing. Still he was joyful beyond measure, beyond mere satisfaction with his lot, beyond cheerful resignation. It would be fair to say that he lived in a permanent state of blissful anticipation for each new moment that God in His infinite wisdom saw fit to send him.

From the moment the little monk was rudely awoken at dawn, sometimes by the application of a soaking rag to his face if his gaoler, the wretched Fleque, was in a particularly foul mood, to when he laid his head on the rude sack of straw that served as his pillow that night, he was the most deeply contented prisoner it would be possible to imagine.

With a view to deflecting unwanted attention, Dromo made a point of appearing to be utterly miserable at all times. On the rare occasions when he was let out of his cell to walk around the castle parapet with the other prisoners, he kept his gaze firmly fixed on the floor, as though praying for salvation. If he caught the eye of another man he would look away, stifling the urge to twinkle merrily in the other fellow's direction. Some time ago he had let his guard down. While pondering a question that had entertained him for some months, for the little monk had a curious nature, given to endless speculations, he had hit upon a solution whilst waiting in line for a bowl of gruel to be handed to him. So delighted was he by the revelation that he could not help but cry out in ecstasy, only avoiding punishment by twisting his features at the last into an agonised grimace, so that the watching guards merely assumed he had caught sight of the soup, a quite disgusting oatmeal and nettle concoction, and let him be. He neither knew nor cared why these other poor devils had been locked up. For all he knew they were each as secretly happy as him, like him only feigning misery.

These events took place long ago, in that period of history we now refer to as the Middle Ages, though the inhabitants of the day would have been hard pressed to know exactly what it was they were in the middle of, in a country whose borders have been redrawn and reimagined many times but which was then a patchwork of independent states and provinces ruled by kings and lords and other self-important folk. Steeped in human rivalry, deceit and treachery, the world outside the little monk's prison cell marched to the throbbing drum of war. But inside, all was calm.

He wanted for nothing. His food was usually brought to him. He had his two prized possessions, the books over which he daily hunched, scribbling and scribing his thoughts as they flashed into his eager mind, along with a quill pen and a regularly renewed supply of ink. All this plus a magnificent view from the tower, to the east across the rooftops of the nearby town of Boroglass and the wide ocean beyond, and to the west, as backdrop, the imposing, imperious mountain range which formed a natural boundary to the province of Metagoria, the land over which King Ludovico II, who also lived in this same castle, reigned.

Of course no mere view, no matter how splendid, could enchant a man, could intoxicate and bewitch him so effectively as Dromo was enchanted, intoxicated, bewitched. For Dromo had a secret, a great treasure that served as his constant, ever-faithful companion. Dromo was a slave to science. He loved to watch and to ponder, and to measure and record his observations. Prison life was colourless, relentlessly drab to the average prisoner. Not to Dromo, who alone was privileged to study the mind of God as revealed to him through the workings of His creation, Nature. The many and various changes that Dromo's small world was subject to in the course of a season, or a day, or indeed an hour, the shadow that traced its slow arc across the walls of his prison cell, its angle of rotation seemingly dependent on the season, the stars in their constellations wheeling in the night sky, these were all evidence of the Mind of God. And each was duly recorded in a weighty ledger that sat in pride of place on its stone shelf. It was labelled *Doctrina* and was specially set aside for these scientific observations. Another book, *Doctrina's* twin, sat alongside. This one was reserved for storytelling and thoughts of a more fanciful nature.

Mortal man must rest, but God never did. For Dromo, the insights into His Mind never ceased. Even in apparent stillness, Dromo found, there is constant, restless movement of the earth and the heavens, movement of a kind that perhaps only a prisoner, or someone paying particularly close attention, can know. And you can be sure that Dromo charted all of it, the position of the sun on the horizon as it rose and set. The mysterious, back-and-forth movement of some stars against the fixed velvet backdrop, juveniles, it seemed, breaking free from their parents' influence. Every observation was lovingly charted and cross-referenced within the pages of *Doctrina*. What could it all mean? Dromo had all the time he needed to ponder that question.

All the time in the world.

---oOo---

Antoine Fleque was a cruel and devious man, ideally suited to his role of gaoler to the little monk. Towering over his charge, despite a deformity of the spine that made him stoop and imparted to him a shuffling, sideways gait, he was a stranger to hygiene and carried about him a permanent rancid stench, as if some evil, decomposing thing had taken up residence in the folds of his filthy tunic. His overripe, rubbery features hung as though suspended from the matted rug of hair above, his bulbous, warty nose, flapping cheeks and protruding eyes all seeming to jostle for prime position on his face as he belched out orders and insults through a haze of spittle and rotten breath. Dromo loved him unconditionally.

Nor was Dromo's tormentor blessed with a great intellect. If it is possible for a man to be both cunning and stupid at the same time, Antoine Fleque achieved such a paradoxical state with ease. Fleque's role in the administration of the castle was quite unclear to Dromo, though it must be said that he had never felt the slightest need to enquire of it. Suffice to say that if there was a lowlier specimen among the King's coterie of servants then Dromo was not aware of that sorry individual's existence. Even the other servants looked down upon this deformed soul, twisted as he was in both body and spirit.

Dromo's circular cell had two openings set deep within the walls, through which the wind would howl on desolate winter nights. These slits in the stone architecture of the castle's southernmost tower were long and narrow, designed to be just wide enough for an archer to fire down upon an invader. If Dromo stood on his desk, which, being a curious monk, he was wont to do from time to time, he was able to look out across the rooftops of neighbouring Boroglass. There was little chance of his falling through the opening, and besides, from his vantage point it was not possible to look straight down, but the aperture did offer a partial view of the castle's ramparts below. At various times of the day Fleque could be spied hurrying here and there, laden with cooking vessels or milk churns, or carrying swords or pikestaffs for the assembled knights, limping and fawning over his superiors, every bit as much a slave to his masters, it seemed, as Dromo was to him. But his principal duty was to bring the daily bowl of kitchen slops and dry bread to the prisoner in the tower, his ascendance of the spiral stone staircase invariably accompanied by a great deal of wheezing and coughing, mixed with the odd curse.

Sometimes he would visit Dromo for no other reason than to antagonise and taunt him. This was one such occasion. It was late in the afternoon and Dromo had lit a candle against the darkening autumn sky that was crowding in upon his frosty abode. As it happened, the juddering flame that danced in the pool of melted wax atop the candle was illuminating his work in more ways than one, for it was this very phenomenon, the conversion of wax into light and heat, that he was studying. He dipped his quill pen in the inkwell on his desk and held it in anticipation above the parchment of his beloved book of doctrine. The other book, the one he had named 'Fabula', lay undisturbed on its stone ledge.

"Why you so round?"

Dromo stared ahead with furrowed brow, absorbed in his work, and made no attempt to answer. The flickering of a candle had always fascinated the monk. He had made some rudimentary notes on the subject before, some time ago. He could refer back to them, but for now he would content himself with simply observing and pondering the phenomenon. What was the nature of the exchange occurring before his eyes between wax, wick and the nimble, excitable, incandescent flame? What was it that spurred this little spark into action as it fed hungrily on – what? The air in the room? For Dromo knew that one could starve a candle to extinction by placing it under a glass. More than this, one must not be fooled by the bright and brave little flame's jaunty appearance, for it burned with a fearsome heat, repelling any attempt to grasp it. And should it come into contact with some material, Dromo knew, it would multiply and grow until, from this tiny seed, a conflagration. Where did the wax go? First it was there, then it was gone. Some fundamental law of God's devising was being demonstrated here, matter itself converting to heat and light before Dromo's wide-open eyes.

Suddenly Fleque's greasy paw shot out, dealing Dromo a sharp blow to the side of the head and causing a drop of ink to quiver, detach itself from the quill and land on the page below, forming an elongated ovoid mark. Dromo flinched, smiled at the inky shape, making a mental note to investigate it further at some point, then quickly rearranged his features into their customary humble state of contrition.

"I say why you round? You round like a ball. Fat. And you don't even eat nothing, your food. Why is this? Why you round?"

It was not strictly a question, at least not one that Fleque needed an answer to. He cared not one little bit whether Dromo ate the crust of bread and thin vegetable stew that he was now pointing at with a stubby, outstretched finger. But he was bored and, being at least notionally a man, as needful of human contact as every other man on the planet, he sought conversation. If he could simultaneously injure Dromo's pride in some way, then so much the better.

"M…my apologies, Antoine," said Dromo. He followed the grubby finger with his eyes to where the food lay congealing in a ray of autumn sunshine, then bowed his head towards his gaoler in an outward gesture of supplication.

"It looks appetising. I will eat presently. It is good of you to remind me that the food is there, Antoine. I had quite forgotten."

Then, remembering that he had been asked a question, Dromo paused for a moment, as on all such occasions he struggled to find the right balance of words to simultaneously convey his misery and disguise his joy.

"Perhaps my roundness is … a punishment," he ventured. "God, in His infinite wisdom, has seen fit to make me this way. Had I not been so sinful as to require imprisonment, I should have been given

17

the body of an Adonis, rather like your own, dear Antoine."

And with this utterance, which surely could not pass as anything but the slyest and most cruel sarcasm, Dromo held his breath. Was this a step too far? Fleque merely shrugged, being very well used to Dromo's downcast eyes and insufferable politeness. If the remark had been intended as an insult, Fleque seemed not to have understood it as such. It may have helped that he did not recognise the name Adonis. At the same time he could not help but enjoy being called Antoine. It was the only time he ever heard his Christian name being spoken aloud in the castle, his own masters preferring to address him as Fleque, if they remembered his name at all. He stared out of the narrow window, lost in a sudden reverie.

The candle burned down slowly towards its demise. A human must leave this world, and a candle, too. But stone, like these castle walls? Must they, too, one day vanish, leaving no trace? Dromo pondered ceaselessly on these questions. Could all men know God's secrets, or had He, in His Infinite Wisdom, decided to bestow this knowledge solely upon His humble servant Dromo? It was true that most men, Antoine Fleque for one, paid no more attention to the guttering of a candle flame than they did to a flea's permanent feasting upon their hides. One burned, one itched. But still. God might open their eyes wide, too, if He so wished, could He not?

All at once Dromo's attention was drawn to a phenomenon even more arresting than the elemental jig of the candle flame. Of all God's works, the monk had never been in doubt that the finest in all creation was man himself. It followed that the greatest sin of all was to pay no heed to another's suffering. What he had thought to be a derisory cough or weary expression of disdain from Antoine proved to be nothing of the sort. He looked across to see that his accuser, his nemesis, his gaoler and tormentor of these numberless years past, was crying. Antoine Fleque's whole body shook as he gulped and gasped for air, holding his breath in an attempt to stem the tide. It was no use. Tears rolled freely down both cheeks, cutting through layers of grime with their cleansing salt tracks. His body arched over, as if to follow the tears in their downward course, and it was then that he gave vent to an unearthly, animal bark of purest grief. Dromo's heart melted at the sound.

"Antoine. My dear Antoine…"

He levered himself from the desk and threw his arms around his gaoler's heaving shoulders. Antoine did not resist the embrace, which only seemed to trigger, or release, yet more powerful bouts of helpless sobbing. There they remained for some time, locked together while the emotion ebbed and flowed to its own rhythm. Antoine continued to buckle, dissolving before Dromo into a puddle of sweat and tears and stink that would have repelled many less kindly folk. But the monk felt not the slightest twinge of revulsion at holding onto him this tightly, nor could he, all men being equal in their hour of greatest need. He whispered, as tenderly as any lover, into Antoine's ear.

"What is it?"

No answer came, so that after a while Dromo repeated the question. Antoine could not speak and in answer could only point out of the window. Dromo followed his outstretched arm, taking in the narrow strip of unruly autumn sky that glowered above. Restless dark clouds swept visibly past, punctured here and there by the late-afternoon sun.

"The clouds?"

19

Antoine shook his head but continued to point. Dromo looked back and this time saw a large formation of birds purposefully making its way overhead, so far away as to be approaching Heaven itself.

"The birds! … Yes. They are heading south for the winter."

Antoine nodded sadly, finally gaining control of his wayward bosom. Finally he spoke, the words escaping his lips between little gasps.

"Mama said … when Antoine is come into the world … it was the same."

"I see."

Antoine's voice, softened by the release of sorrow, had taken on the cadence of a child. Now it was Dromo's turn to fight back tears as he pictured the infant Fleque feeding hungrily at his mother's breast, or gurgling happily on her knee, unmarked by deformity, long before he fell prey to drudgery and servitude, and the many other privations and humiliations that this world had in store for Antoine Fleque. He gently pulled away from the embrace, seeming neither embarrassed at his exuberant expression of emotion, nor angry at Dromo's intervention. He merely sat for a while, staring inwardly, oblivious to any other presence in the room. When their eyes finally met and Dromo spoke there was a teasing, almost shy quality to his words.

"So then. What are you telling me, Antoine? Am I to understand … that it's your birthday?"

---o0o---

He stood in line with the other prisoners, heads lowered as they waited their turn to receive a ladle of watery gruel into their chipped wooden bowls. The food looked and tasted bad but it was at least hot, and this weekly ritual was looked forward to by most, especially now, with the days growing ever chillier, and warm summer nights fast fading in memory. Dromo was normally content to keep his gaze fixed upon his sandals like the others, but today was different. Today he had a plan.

So moved had Dromo been by Antoine's sudden outburst that from this point on he had become obsessed with finding a way to celebrate his gaoler's birthday, or at the very least mark it. Of course there was no way of knowing the exact date of this happy occasion since, with the exception of royal persons and the nobility in general, few of the common folk in this far-off time kept track of the days, beyond knowing when Sunday, the Lord's Day, came around. Indeed most would scarcely be aware of the changing seasons, save those who worked the land, and Antoine was not among their number, being merely servant to a servant, the lowest of the low. It would do no good to enquire of Antoine's mother, so that she may apprise them of the actual date. She was most likely dead, and, should that be the case, there was no need to prolong Antoine's suffering by reminding him of the fact. It hardly mattered, the migrating birds having heralded the event in such timely fashion, but Dromo had become like a man possessed. For Antoine's sake, and for every downtrodden soul living in the castle and beyond, he would risk all to mark this day.

Here was a pretty conundrum: a man who owned nothing trying to give a present to one equally without means. At last, unable to solve the riddle, Dromo came to the conclusion that he would have to call on the services of another, one as rich as he and Antoine were poor. Thus, when it came to his turn for gruel, he put his plan into action.

He began to hum a merry tune, which he accompanied with a little jig that set his round belly on a wobble. He sniffed at the steaming grey liquid before him, lifted his head, and with the broadest grin on his face pronounced it the most wonderfully aromatic food he had ever smelled. Raising his arms to Heaven he asked the prisoners queueing with him to join in a prayer of thanks for the meal they were about to receive. When this was met with blank stares of incomprehension he began to giggle. To his surprise there was great relief in dropping the mask of humility he had always worn and the giggles quickly gave way to uncontrolled snorts, which then turned to howls of laughter. Though perhaps only one tenth of the joy he truly felt in his heart it was nevertheless an honest expression of pure happiness and contentment.

Quite promptly and wholly as planned, two guards roughly seized him and hauled him away.

---oOo---

King Ludovico II sat in the throne room awaiting his audience with the prisoner, all the while adjusting the folds of his opulent robes, trimmed with the softest rabbit fur, in an effort to create what he deemed the most compelling regal impression. This was not in the least necessary, especially given the lowly status of the miscreant he was about to admit to this most hallowed of sanctuaries, but the king was burdened with a somewhat nervous temperament, and thus prone to all manner of petty foibles of an all too human nature. It was for this reason that he kept all contact with the world outside the castle walls strictly to a minimum, trusting all affairs of state to his few intimate advisors. This policy had served him surpassingly well in the early years of his reign, his absence from the body politic spawning, by some happy chance, the rumour that he was a fearsome and forbidding despot, who would not suffer fools even to enter his sight. Alas, as time went on and the whispering intensified, he found he could not venture out at all, for fear that he would not be able to live up to the impression of himself that had been created. And so, in some sense, and by degrees, he had become as much a prisoner in the castle as the little monk.

His father, Ludovico, had been an altogether different creature, a truly valiant, brave warrior who had led his armies through numerous conquests to establish the sprawling kingdom over which his son now held dominion. Victorious to the last, he ultimately fell in battle, struck down by an enemy axe. His troops, seeing him so diminished, had been spurred on by rage, and won the day in his absence. Sainthood for King Ludovico had followed as night follows day.

It was perhaps no coincidence that in life the first Ludovico had been a greatly more contented man than the second would turn out, being all the happier for never having relied upon an inheritance himself. That which the father forged with his bare hands, which he fought and died for so gallantly, the son, having played no part in its creation, looked upon as the heaviest of burdens, a duty to be carried out in perpetuity. Notwithstanding the king's malaise, and arguably adding to it, was the fact that Metagoria was quite easily defended. Its natural boundary of the impenetrable mountain range, running for hundreds of miles inland from the coast, made invasion from the West impossible, and the expanse of ocean to the east meant that an invasion fleet stood little chance of mounting a surprise attack.

23

Preparations were in place for defending Ludovico's realm by the full force of his standing army at the first sign of a sail on the horizon. Further along the coast, in both directions, could be found hostile, warring tribes: to the north the savage Mendicans, and to the south the incomprehensible Szarks. The Metagorians traded wool and many other goods with both, forming fragile, uneasy alliances that had somehow held for decades.

The throne room was just that, a wide space dressed in oak beneath a vaulted ceiling, its walls bedecked with emblems and trophies from ancient wars, flags of conquered nations, coats of arms and ceremonial weapons. Otherwise the room was bereft of furniture, save the throne itself, rising proudly from a sea of grey slate. The large and imposing doors swung slowly open and two guards entered, dwarfing the prisoner who shuffled forward between them in his tattered monk's habit, stealing furtive looks around him. The guards approached the throne, bowed, then at the barest of gestures from Ludovico turned on their heels and left the room, closing the doors behind them. Dromo swayed a little, reeling from the imposing architecture as much as from the scrutiny of the king, looking smaller, rounder than ever as he stood there alone. He had never laid eyes upon this room before, nor had he so much as glimpsed his sovereign and Lord.

The king spoke with a dry, indifferent air, tugging at a loose thread on his sleeve.

"There has been a disturbance. Something to do with your food?"

Dromo opened his mouth, then closed it again. A little time passed, though it seemed eternal.

"Why do you not offer up thanks to be in my presence?"

The words were meant sarcastically but they still hit home for

Dromo. Suddenly he collapsed to his knees, clasping his hands before him in supplication.

"Sire, forgive me. I do give thanks, but my performance in the kitchen was mere pretence. I needed to speak with you on a delicate matter, and could see no other way of gaining an audience with you … Sire."

Not knowing quite what was expected of him, he crouched there, awaiting further developments. Eventually Ludovico gestured for him to stand. Dromo scrambled to his feet.

"I'm told you occupy the southern tower, that you have been confined there for crimes against this realm. Furthermore, you have been resident as long as any living soul can remember. Is this true?"

Dromo nodded gravely, then launched into his practised speech.

"My Lord, with your permission, I wish to advise you that one of your loyal subjects, a servant by the name of Antoine Fleque…"

"Why were you imprisoned?"

This came as a surprise, since Dromo had always been too preoccupied to seek an answer to that question. Surely there must have been records kept? Had there been no trial? No sentence? Dromo had no recollection of his initial incarceration. Along with the king's advisors, he could not place himself anywhere but in his beloved cell. Furthermore, try as he might to picture a scene that did not involve his cell, his gaoler and his two mighty books *Doctrina* and *Fabula*, he could not do it. There didn't seem to be a time before these great and wonderful gifts had been bestowed upon him. There simply was no 'before'.

He did, however, know the reason why he had been locked away. This much had been handed down to him by none other than Antoine

Fleque.

"Murders, my Lord, most grievous and villainous murders." He added quickly, "… Antoine is a simple soul, who asks for nothing. Yet within his breast there beats the heart of a man. And it has come to my attention…"

"Do you repent these deeds?"

This put the already confused Dromo in a further quandary. Never having encountered royalty before, he had no knowledge of the proper etiquette or rules of engagement, chief among them being that a prisoner does not converse freely with a king but rather waits upon the king's pleasure until such time as he is dismissed. He nodded slowly, keeping his eyes fixed upon the dark slate floor of the throne room with its honeycomb pattern of tiles stretching in all directions.

"I do repent them, Sire." He bowed his head.

Honeycomb, the shape beloved of bees, was God's most discretely functional, most beautiful lattice, one of the sacred pillars of geometry. It had always fascinated Dromo. Here was a six-sided figure, a hexagon, so simply constructed with a straight rule and compass, yet endowed with the power to conjoin harmoniously with its brothers, arm-in-arm, as it were, and pave a surface with no boundary. Dromo stared at the floor. As mighty as the throne room was, the little hexagon was mightier. This great chamber at the heart of the castle, secure behind massive walls of stone a metre thick, could hold armies at bay. But these same walls could not stop the little hexagon's march to infinity. Where the slate tiles could be stopped in their tracks, the shapes themselves persisted in their course, their form unchanging. Dromo had written of similar shapes, had traced them in his book, *Doctrina*. Of the regular ones, God in His infinite wisdom had created only three, of which the hexagon reigned supreme, the others being a triangle of equal sides and a square. Through these tiles, these shapes, God was trying to tell Dromo something of consuming importance.

All at once it came, with the impact of a crossbow bolt to the chest: God spoke to him with the answer to the riddle. He almost gasped aloud at the revelation. It took the king's stern voice to break the spell.

"Did you hear what I said?"

Dromo blinked furiously, desperate to hold onto God's divine message in the geometry of the floor tiles but suddenly aware that he must also complete his mission for Antoine. More than this, he had offended Ludovico. He had no idea what had been said to him, so decided in the moment to continue with his plan unabashed.

"Yes. I was saying … Antoine, you see. The birds, they… flying south for… At his mother's knee, and this means that…"

"You are pardoned."

The terrible words broke through his babble at last, and nothing after this would be the same for the little monk, though his mouth continued to form words.

"It's … his birthday. … You see."

"I said you are pardoned." Ludovico expressed only the slightest irritation at having to repeat himself. There was a long moment when Dromo stood frozen to the spot, staring ahead like a lunatic. The king grew bored and settled back into the folds of his cloak.

"We are setting you free."

He waved Dromo away as he would a fly at dinner.

---oOo---

A discourse of the most arresting and profound nature on the subject of free will took place between one Edouard Apery, Duc de Pomerance, a wealthy landowner, and a penniless vagabond by the name of Palini, beside a river. The rich man had happened upon Palini as he journeyed on horseback on some official business, and their first encounter could well have resulted in the death of one or other of the two men, if not both. That summer having been unusually wet in this part of the world, the river had swollen and burst its banks in many places. Thus the Duc had been forced to follow its winding course in search of a suitable point to cross the still turbulent waters. Palini had been lying on his side, half-asleep, in some long grass and got the fright of his life when the Duc's handsome white horse reared up above him, very nearly unseating its rider, who, had he not clung to the reins with grim determination, would surely have ended in the river. Palini, for his part, avoided the horse's thrashing hooves by the narrowest of margins.

"You!" the Duc shouted angrily, finally bringing his agitated steed under control. "What do you think you're doing there, you idle fellow?"

He went so far as to halfway draw his sword, but then changed his mind on seeing his assailant in plain view. Here was no cutpurse or highwayman, but the meanest, most impoverished of wretches, barely clothed, looking half-starved and quite unencumbered by weapons of any kind.

Startled, Palini instinctively blurted out an apology, though it would be hard to argue where his fault lay. If the bank of this river had ever been used to guide travellers in their course, then the pathway had long since been obliterated by storms and rising water. But it is a universal truth that a man on horseback, especially one draped in the finest vestments, as was the Duc de Pomerance, can often inspire in even the highest-born soul a subservient manner, if he happens to be on foot. Indeed, one of the great advantages of this saddled and domesticated beast, were it only to be admitted, has less to do with transportation than with its owner's desire to look down upon his fellow men from a superior vantage point. Palini was a tall man, with angular features and sharp bones barely covered by translucent skin that shone with an unearthly pallor. His great height was accentuated by the leanness of his skeletal frame, yet still he had to crane his neck to look the other man in the eye.

"What's the meaning of this? A poacher, is it? Is that what you're up to?"

"I... If it please you, no, Sire. I was s... sleeping," stammered Palini, trying vainly to distance himself from the makeshift rod and line where it lay half on the grass, half-propped against a rock. The rod had been fashioned from a willow branch. A trailing thread hung from the end of it and disappeared into the sparkling, fast-moving water. Had one looked closely, it would have been apparent that the thread was of the same colour as Palini's worn woollen topcoat, which had clearly started its life as a much longer garment. Where it might once have reached to his knees, now it barely covered his hollow stomach above the protruding hip bones.

"You are far more danger to your fellow man lying there than to any fish, wastrel! Get off the path! If you must sit, sit by a tree where you can be seen." And he added, unnecessarily, "And you will address me as 'my Lord'."

"Yes, my Lord."

Palini glanced around. There were a great many trees to choose from, this being a densely forested area for miles around. He had been wandering, perhaps in circles, it was impossible to say, for many weeks, too many to count, travelling by night to keep himself warm, and only resting when sleep overtook him, as it had in the late-afternoon sunshine. Edouard Apery was the first two-legged being he had set his eyes upon in some while, and he could not help but be impressed and a little overawed in the presence of a nobleman.

The Duc climbed down from his horse, settling the matter of their differing heights at once. Now it was his turn to look up at Palini, which he did with undisguised scorn.

"Count yourself very fortunate that I am not the owner of these lands but merely passing through, or you would surely hang for your insolence."

Palini nodded respectfully, mindful of the charge of poaching that this rich man might bring upon him. He himself owned nothing, depending on the fruits of the forest, and whatever fish or fowl that he could snare for sustenance. He was no stranger to towns and villages. When coming upon one he would barter for food, his only coin being his strong back and willingness to work at menial tasks. But he preferred the silence of the forest, finding its inhabitants to be more forgiving of a stranger's presence than their human counterparts. Moreover, he knew the penalties for vagrancy, so was ever mindful of the need to keep moving and where possible stay out of sight.

The Duc led his horse to the water's edge where it drank deeply, snorting and shaking its mane to rid itself of the flies and ticks that massed at the water's edge. He took a leather-clad drinking vessel from his saddlebag and briefly swigged at it, then dipped his fine silk handkerchief into the clear water. Wringing out the excess he dabbed at his forehead and neck, which were grimy with the sweat of a hard day's riding, then replenished his water bottle from the swift-moving river. Behind him the sun was setting over the treetops, its defiant last rays piercing through the gloom of the forest, illuminating bush, bark and fern alike with fiery haloes. It would soon be dark. His horse would have to rest and this was as good a place as he was likely to find to make camp for the night. His quest to find a crossing had failed, but the rain clouds had cleared and some stars were already showing visible in the pale blue sky, now tinged with pink. Perhaps by morning the waters would have receded and he could safely continue on his journey. Looking about him, he was almost surprised to find Palini still patiently standing there, as though awaiting orders. He waved his hand dismissively.

"Well, then, what are you waiting for? Be off with you."

Palini bent down to collect his fishing rod, then retrieved a bundle of some rough sacking that he'd been using as a pillow. He took a few steps in the direction of the forest, then hesitated and turned back towards Edouard. A benign, questioning look, almost a smile, crossed his face. The Duc watched him keenly, one hand straying cautiously towards the hilt of his sword. It was not uncommon for a man of breeding to be left for dead in such a densely wooded area as this, his horse confiscated along with his purse and his fine clothes. Furthermore, he did not underestimate his opponent, knowing full well how hunger and desperation could endow such a man, as gaunt as he was, with the strength of ten should the occasion arise.

And what better opportunity than out here in this green and russet wilderness, the trees hunched over to shed their blood-red autumn leaves? Edouard had shown himself willing to overlook Palini's crime of poaching. He had not the time or the inclination to march him to the nearest village or town and turn him over to the local magistrate for punishment. To this degree he felt he had shown great lenience. But this alone was no safeguard against his throat being slit with his own cold steel as he slept. No, it would be better to despatch this defenceless creature here and now, or at the very least drive him away and with the Duc's horse refreshed put a few more miles between himself and the possibility of a bloody demise at the ruffian's hands. He almost cried out as the ruffian suddenly stepped forward. Palini, sensing the danger, was quick to reassure him.

"No, my Lord. I only wish to share with you…"

And with that, he proffered the bundle, laying it on the ground at his feet. Then, squatting down, and showing his open palms to Edouard to reassure him, he delicately unfurled the rough material. Not until the contents of the parcel were wholly revealed did the Duc relax his grip on the hilt of his sword. There, nestled together on a patch of darkening river water, and glistening with a purple sheen in the dying light, lay two of the plumpest, freshest trout that the Duc de Pomerance had ever seen.

---oOo---

Palini had not always been a vagrant, but he had forever carried about him an air of loneliness and separation from the world. If it could be said of him that he possessed one thing and one thing alone, it would be a stubborn and enduring inability to possess any one thing at all, be it material wealth, peace of mind or, for the better part of his life, a calling. There are men for whom, whatever comes within their grasp, whatever they touch upon in the course of their lives, invariably fails to return their grip, and Palini was one such unfortunate. Even the food he ate would not adhere to his bones for he never gained any weight, though at various times in his life he had known feasting as well as famine.

Like many souls then and since, he had been born into stark, nameless poverty. At least we can assume as such, since records were not kept in these times and he himself had only the scantest recollection of his beginning. No parents or guardian to speak of, no one to soothe his infant brow or calm his raging adolescent humours. He seemed always to have been moving, his prime motivation being the next meal, however humble. Hunger was the one call to action that could be eternally relied upon, and Palini answered with the greatest enthusiasm. More than this, the ingestion of meat and drink brought him as close as he ever came to a sense of belonging to this earth. Cheese, wine and bread when he could barter for them, olives plucked from the tree, small beer, the carcass of a guinea fowl slowly roasted over a fire of dried juniper branches; these provided his only consolation. Food was his comforter, his guardian, his only friend, and every move he made was in some way to seek it out.

But food alone cannot sustain a man indefinitely. For while his stomach may be gratified, his soul might still hunger. And this aching void will beguile him, blighting his very existence, spurring him on to greater excesses of gluttony, in the mistaken belief that the next meal will finally complete him, finally satisfy his craving and fill the emptiness at his core. Palini had not yet learned this truth.

He had been married once, very happily, to a miller's daughter. As a youth he had been darkly handsome, and his good looks drew the attention of numerous young females who, admiring his upright stance, lean body and strong back, often competed with each other to win his favour. With the bloom of youth upon him and a soft shading of beard accentuating his strong jawline, his gruff, unyielding manner spoke to them of quiet masculine power and hidden virtue. Not for the first time was a troubled soul with little in the way of conversation mistaken for a great and noble spirit, for there is no stronger spell than the one cast by nature to ensure the continuance of the species, that being physical beauty. Palini enjoyed many dalliances and sweet, sun-kissed rendezvous with the gentler sex, but the matter of his low birth and itinerant ways could not be disguised forever, and these affairs of the heart invariably came to nought, until one day, enticed by the smell of baking bread, he spied a maiden selling loaves by a millstream. The maiden's name was Margery, and when she smiled at him Palini felt his heart give a lurch and his tongue, never prone to overuse in the first instance, set like glue in his mouth. He bought warm, scented bread encased in a layer of brown flour that fell from her plump fingers like fine rain when she pressed the loaf into his open palms. Before the flour had settled on the earth their courtship, at least in Palini's mind, had begun.

Margery was pretty and laughed easily, with a sound like a peal of church bells. The slightest touch of her skin gave Palini a sense of comfort that he had never known. To watch her at her workplace, moving with an effortless grace as she went about her duties, filled him with thoughts of woodsmoke and warm blankets, peace and a full belly. Along with Jon, her father, and his assistants she rose before dawn to begin the process of turning wheat grains into flour, and after the simplest of ceremonies at which a local priest blessed their union, Palini was to join them. Thus with a stammered vow did the man who could not own a thing come into possession, all too briefly, of a wife. In the evening there was dancing and a great deal of mead, which the bride's father had brewed himself for the occasion, was imbibed. Palini joined in the revelry, but for once had little appetite for food or wine. Not one for dancing, he sat to one side of the proceedings, watching with fascination the gyrations of his new bride as she jigged and twirled, marvelling at her lack of guile, at her completeness, the ease with which she indulged herself in the simplest of life's pleasures. She beamed at him as she passed, mistaking his guarded smile for exhaustion and contentment combined.

And for a while he was content. His new family were glad of the vigour that he brought to their enterprise, their efforts along with their profits more than doubled by the sweat of his brow, the heft of his shoulders as he carried sacks of grain back and forth. In the evenings he would sit holding hands with Margery and watch as the sun sank behind a hill, throwing colours into the sky like a petulant child. Then to bed, for another day would dawn all too soon, and the ritual would begin anew. He helped with the maintenance of the mill itself, mending broken sails when necessary or greasing its moving parts with goose fat. He milked the one cow that his father-in-law owned, collected eggs from their hens, then in the afternoons chopped wood or gathered kindling for the oven which needed to be set every morning at first light for the day's baking. Hard work was gratifying, not merely for the food it placed on the table but for its ability to staunch, if not extinguish, his vast capacity for doubt. For all that Margery was married to Palini, he was married to the notion that happiness only served as warning for the sorrow that must inevitably follow. Woman, in his world view, was a free spirit, the purest embodiment of goodness, where man was duplicitous and plagued by demons. The attentions of Palini's demons had been hard enough for him to counter when he had nothing. How much harder did they clutch at him now that there was something beyond precious to lose?

Not long after they were married, Margery began to complain of nausea upon waking. It took no time at all for the women of the village to ascertain that she was pregnant with not one but two babies, twin boys, identical in all respects. How the elderly midwife in question was able to make such a detailed prediction was at that time, as it would be today, a mystery akin to magic in the eyes of the menfolk present. Be that as it may, the babies would be born into gentle summer, after the waxing and waning of nine moons, and the prospect generated much excitement at the mill by the stream. In time there would be two strong and handsome young men to share the burden of the daily chores at the bakery. Jon could not be prouder of his daughter, nor Palini of his wife. But along with the excitement came the inevitable worries that accompany the anticipation of a life-changing event. Margery became increasingly flustered and distracted as the weeks went by, afraid that she would lose her figure to such an extent that her husband would no longer find her attractive. In turn Palini, no stranger to doubt as we have seen, confided to her in intimate moments that he would not be a good father, that the boys would be marked by his melancholy disposition, that she would not have love enough for two boys and a husband, so would in due course choose them over him. So the marital dance continued with each insistent that the other's love would not survive, while his or her own would stand firm. As so often happens, God in His infinite wisdom had made other plans for these two.

Margery was alone when the first stab of pain struck with the force of cold steel through her abdomen. She was fetching water from the well and her first thought was that she had overloaded the pail and should have made two trips instead of one. The strain of carrying such a heavy load must have caused the spasm. Being only six moons into her pregnancy, she had no cause to believe the twins were on their way until a second thrust of the lance, bigger and more agonising than the first, left her gasping like a landed fish. She collapsed and had been unconscious for a while before they found her. There followed many hours of fraught but hopeless endeavours to save the poor woman. There was less concern for the twin boys who were understood to be forfeit, since they could not possibly survive the trauma of such an early entry into the world. Though every available female was rushed from the nearby village to lend a hand, they had in the end nothing to offer poor Margery but their prayers. Her agonised cry took every ounce of her strength, along with her life. Jon and Palini stood by, as mute and helpless to intervene as two empty husks of corn.

As for the babies, one had died inside her womb, the other was lifted out after a brief struggle, looking more animal than human, with eyes black and unformed, his mouth agape as he struggled for air, his limbs as fragile as a fledgling's wings. He was too weak to cry out, having barely strength enough to lift his head. The women crossed themselves, wrapped the boy in a shawl and brought him near to the fire. Palini thought momentarily that they might be about to give his son to the flames, so made a move to protest, but they assured him they were merely warming the tiny creature. He would not last much longer, they told his weeping father. It was left to them merely to pray for his soul. Palini did not pray, but instead took his tiny son in his arms. A single tear dropped from his eye, anointing the baby's head. He did not think that he could bear witness to the boy's passing, but he would do it for the sake of his wife, now a mother, but lost to him forever.

---oOo---

"Why are you so thin?"

He had watched his companion devour his supper, the sweet flesh of the trout bursting with its juices, skin crisp from the fire, as though it were his last, stopping only to wipe his mouth with the sleeve of his shabby tunic, and all the while recounting, between mouthfuls, the story of his wife, their courtship, brief life together and her subsequent death in childbirth.

"…You eat well enough, my friend."

Palini had no answer to the question, and merely shrugged.

Edouard Apery was not a cruel man, despite the rudeness he had formerly displayed towards this humble vagrant. In fact he prided himself on his fair-mindedness, his ability to see in others both good and bad, regardless of their status in the world. This was due to his own journey through life, which had begun in circumstances not very much less humble than Palini's. He knew himself to be a fine judge of character, so by this time had given up his initial doubts, his fear that the man in rags before him might slit his throat while he was sleeping, and shared with him the contents of his wine bottle. Even despite this, the reference to Palini's gaunt and famished frame had been an insensitive one, a sad reflection of many a rich man's view of his impoverished neighbour, then and now.

Perhaps he knew it, for the Duc took another swig, then passed the bottle to Palini, grunting with the effort of raising himself from his bedroll. Both men were quite drunk, the blanket of night by now firmly closed around them. Eerie nocturnal sounds pierced the unforgiving darkness but each man felt safe, cocooned in the orange glow of the campfire, fortified against the evening chill, their bellies replete with succulent fish and good red wine. Palini tossed a handful of dry twigs onto the fire. It crackled in the heat, sending a small explosion of sparks flying up to join the bejewelled sky. He settled back against a tree and closed his eyes, offering up silent thanks for this brief moment of companionship. Edouard saw his lips moving quietly and knew at once that Palini was praying. He half-chuckled to himself.

"My dear Palini," he said with an expansive, theatrical gesture, "what a merry time we have had of it, dining and telling each other stories. The Good Lord has provided well for us this night."

"Indeed he has, my Lord."

"We must rest now, we must sleep as soundly as two bears in winter, content that when we wake, our saviour will have set another feast before us, to break our fast."

"Yes, Sire. Goodnight."

"Goodnight."

Palini gathered his threadbare coat around him and settled deeper into the pile of fallen leaves that would be his bed for the night. Despite the recent rain, the canopy of trees above had kept the leaves tolerably dry, and now they acted like a welcome cushion for the long limbs he folded around himself. He sank down and waited for the soothing balm of sleep, but it seemed that the Duc de Pomerance had not yet finished with him. Edouard gave a low growl of a laugh, more contemptuous than jovial, and spat into the fire, which hissed back angrily.

"You cannot truly believe that, can you? What man could be so foolish?"

Palini was confused. He had innocently assumed the Duc's words to be sincere.

"Sire...?"

"...That you are a part of God's plan, and you need only wait to see what lies in store? Come come now."

"But I do. I do believe it."

"Then, my poor, dear Palini, you deserve to be as poor as you are."

Palini looked bewildered. He had surely said nothing that could give offence. The Duc sighed impatiently.

"Tell me this, if you will. Did God place those two fishes in your path so that you might share them with me this evening?"

"He did, Sire, and I do praise Him for it."

"But who did the fishing, and who the sharing? I well recall bidding you be gone, on pain of death. I showed you my blade, but you tarried, and we have enjoyed a fine supper. Was this also God's work?"

Palini blinked at this, made as though to speak, but could not find words. The Duc continued, scarcely pausing for breath.

"It was your decision, not God's. You exercised your own free will, without which I would have gone hungry. I am most indebted to you.

The Lord God played no part."

"But … there were two fishes, one for each of us. It seemed only right that …"

The Duc stilled Palini's tongue with a raised hand. He was sitting bolt upright now. He spoke with a passion that Palini found unsettling.

"This is how so many are undone. Mark me, and listen well if you would better understand God's plan. He has given you the right to choose your path. And know this, it will be your path, Palini, not His, for should you choose to sit here by this river for eternity, you may be rewarded with a good meal tomorrow, as you have tonight, but then again should the fishes not rise to your bait, you might well starve. Either way, it is foolish beyond measure to believe that God decided your fate. It was a choice you yourself made."

Palini thought hard. The concept under discussion was far beyond his powers of reason.

"This … free will that you speak of. I cannot see how we are free."

"And that is why you are enslaved."

"My destiny is preordained."

"This I believe to be true. But it is true because you believe it to be so. Your choice, once again."

The Duc leaned forward now across the fire with an almost crazed expression. His face and neck shone red from the glow of the dying embers, giving him a devilish appearance. Palini thought he might burst into flames.

"Your destiny is what you make it. God demands you seek it out, not wait for it to be revealed to you. That is why you have free will. If I had not seen this for myself as a young boy, I would be the one now foraging for roots and berries, skulking in this forest, waiting by a river for a fish to tug at my line, leaving all to chance, accepting all with a heavy heart, since all was God's will, and nought of my doing. Answer me this: if you have not free will, then what have you?"

This time, Palini had his answer. He lowered his eyes in shame.

"I have nothing, Sire, and it has plagued me my whole life."

"But you have free will. This is God's gift to every man, his only gift, and I have seen you exercise it. Else why risk death to give food to a stranger? Could I not have killed you and taken both fishes for myself?"

Palini's uncertainty was equal in measure to the Duc's righteous anger.

"It may be that I have done so, that I have risked all, but if I have, I cannot say why. … Perhaps, then, it was my destiny to meet my end here, at your hands."

"And mine to bring you swiftly to that end, as it did occur to me to do. But look… I stayed my hand. Even when you offered me the food I could have run you through and enjoyed my meal in peace. But I chose, mark you, I *chose,* a different path. And here we are, good Palini, digesting happily together. By offering me the fishes, you altered my affections toward you. So that now we are brothers."

Now it was Palini's turn to ask a question.

"How can I know what is my destiny?"

"You must watch for the signs. God sends them to us at every turn but we must be alert to their presence. That is the difference between us. I am ever alert, and when the signs appear to me, I seize upon them without hesitation. You see?"

Palini did not see. Things happened, people died, others were born. There was no pattern, at least none which mortal man could know. It was for God to know these things, for Him to give or to take according to His divine plan. And His plan was for Palini to be poor and outcast, having lost his family, one by one. How could it be otherwise?

The Duc de Pomerance yawned, and nestled back onto his bed. He gazed up at the night sky for a while, and his voice when he eventually spoke was drowsy and far-off sounding.

"I cannot know my destiny. But I have tried throughout my life to force nature to bend to my will. As a consequence I have fought many battles, emerging for the most part victorious. I have won and lost great wealth, but always honourably, always in the pursuit of valour. This I believe to be God's plan, that I should take his glorious gift and fashion it to my own ends. There lies my destiny. ... I could have been a poor man, like your good self. ... Yes. I could have been."

His words began to trail away as sleep overtook him.

"Be sure to create your destiny, for if you don't, the Lord will make you live your wretched life over and over until you do. Watch for the signs, Palini. ... Watch for the signs."

He began to snore softly. Palini lay himself down, the Duc's extraordinary idea resounding in his mind. He could not understand it fully, but yet he knew somehow that a great truth had been revealed to him. The forest was quite still now. Like Palini it seemed to hold its breath. The only sound was the gentle purring of the wind that moved the trees above him, and the rustle of the leaves as he shifted his position, preparing to sleep. But sleep would not come.

Early the next morning Edouard Apery, Duc de Pomerance, awoke to the sound of birdsong. He rose stiffly, stretched and yawned, then looked around for Palini, who was nowhere nearby. He washed his face quickly in the chill, clear water of the river, saddled his horse and rode away, the events of the previous evening giving him not the slightest pause for thought.

Meanwhile, Palini, having spent a restless night, was already on the road, no longer a wanderer, now a man in search of his destiny.

2
NOVEMBER

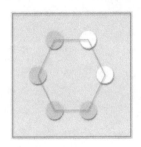

There could be no doubt. Three regular shapes, the square, the triangle with equal sides and the hexagon, these three held the key to all of creation. God had made a gift of them to mankind, and by divine decree it had been granted that the little monk, Dromo, alone among men, should be vouchsafed their meaning. The dawn found him hunched over his desk, *Doctrina* open before him. A blank page gleamed invitingly for the quill pen to inseminate it with this blessed truth, a truth that Dromo knew, beyond mere understanding, would free all men from their mortal bonds, would end all human suffering, would bring peace, finally, to the world. He had only to recall the flash of insight that had come upon him with such sublime clarity in the throne room.

But he could not do it.

His quill remained aloft, trembling in his hand, helplessly denied its divine destiny. The parchment below thirsted in vain for its magical rendezvous with ultimate truth. Just a few strokes of the pen were all it would have taken to deliver the answer to a mystery that his fellow men had puzzled over since antiquity. But where Dromo had seen all with perfect clarity, for that elusive instant, his mind was now a partial fog, as vague as the early morning mist that clung to the rooftops of Boroglass and slowly wound its way around the castle, forming a semi-opaque, milky shroud. Here and there he could make out a flagstone, a rampart, some tiling on a roof, appearing then fading from view. And in the midst of it all, a familiar Janus-faced gargoyle, one that he had always loved, now seemed to mock him, its double-sided leering features showing now mirth at his predicament, now withering scorn.

He had spent a sleepless night since the king's pardon had shaken him to his very core. He was to be set free. No sooner had the king uttered the words that damned the little monk for all eternity than he had dismissed him. A single clap of the king's hands had summoned the guards, and Dromo was deposited, shaking, into the gnarled hands of Antoine Fleque. His gaoler had evidently been apprised of the situation.

"Lucky monk."

Dromo had barely been aware of Fleque's taunts as they wound their way back through the dark tunnels and passageways of the castle's interior. He had ascended the spiral stairway to his lofty cell as though in a dream. The details of his coming ejection from the only home he knew had not been made clear to him, if indeed they had been decided upon. Was he to be mercilessly thrown out upon the hour? At the next full moon perhaps? The first and most alarming of those two options had now fortunately come and gone. The second would have another twenty revolutions of the earth to wait. This was still far too soon for Dromo. It was impossible to even contemplate leaving his cell. For one thing there was *Doctrina*, his sacred volume of astonishing proofs, sublime equations, dark and powerful and wonderful secrets that now lay open before him. How could it be finished? And what of the other volume, *Fabula,* with which he was equally engaged? Would he be allowed to take them with him? And even if he could, where on earth would he work? How could he continue his observations without a supply of ink, without the food, however meagre the ration, that was brought to him daily? He would be helpless in the world out there, beyond these sturdy castle walls.

Antoine Fleque, having not been party to the king's decision, having never, in fact, been party to any decision that had ever been made by anyone, could not help. There had been no further mention of the circumstances of his birth, still less of his loud and luminous descent into despair. The news had dispelled any thoughts of birthdays, and done nothing whatever to improve Antoine's mood. He evidently had some issues with the king's pardon of someone he had come to know as his prisoner and therefore, to some extent, his property.

"Lucky monk," he said again, closely watching Dromo at his desk. A cable of drool made its way slowly from his lower lip. He was quite unaware of its progress.

"Why they not ask me? They should ask Antoine if the monk can go. I say no, keep him locked up. He no good. He kill many men. Bad monk. Keep him here with Antoine."

Looking across at Fleque for the first time since they had arrived back in his cell together, Dromo's heart burst with love for his impoverished guardian, this shambling, deformed giant whose only friends were the keys that swung from his belt, this drooling dunce who was blind to the treasures that God in His infinite wisdom had spread out before him like so many jewels on a velvet cushion. Once again, Dromo wanted to embrace Antoine, this time for the words he had just spoken. Keep him locked up. Keep him here with Antoine. Yes, yes and a thousand times yes. But Dromo had practised his deception too well. All the while he had been imprisoned, and how long remained the deepest mystery, he had feigned misery. Was he now to throw his arms around his gaoler and beg for his continued incarceration? The stub of candle sat upon his desk in a pool of molten wax, its happy flame long extinguished. Now it was Dromo's mind that flickered and danced, consuming the air in his cell with its unravelling, nameless horrors.

They could not free him. He had killed. Might he not kill again? He couldn't imagine doing so, but then he couldn't imagine living at all, not out there, amongst wild animals and men with pikestaffs and muskets, men who waged war, drank and fought. Not out there in the mist and fog of these dark, late autumn days with their promise of winter frost, chill winds that could lash at the face and hands, water forming into shards of ice to drop to the ground like falling spears. His life was to observe these events, not to be consumed by them. Were he to set foot outside the castle, he would surely perish on the instant, from the shock of it. Keep him here. Yes, keep him here, safe, with Antoine.

The two men held each other's gaze. As to what passed between them who can say? The oversized, evil-smelling guard was clearly resentful of his charge's newfound freedom, suspecting nothing, while the small, round monk silently pleaded to be allowed to stay. Neither man could reveal his true intention to the other, though Dromo naturally possessed more information on the matter than his hapless gaoler. How could he confide in Antoine Fleque? To do so would be to admit that he had perpetrated a lie all this time.

As they sat there, each locked in thought, the rope of spittle hanging from Fleque's lower lip grew longer still. When its owner gently shook his head it swung slowly back and forth. Watching it brought a shred of comfort to Dromo's troubled soul, for it turned his mind back mercifully to his studies.

He had been working with pendula for some while, since

managing to affix the cord from his monk's habit to an overhead beam in his cell, itself no mean feat for such a small and rotund monk. Once attached he had weighted the other end of the cord to his bronze drinking goblet and set it swinging, thereafter to record its motion back and forth, charting his observations in terms of the cord's length, the time it took to make one full swing and return to its original position, and the height from which it began its descent. From these simple observations Dromo had come to the remarkable conclusion that a pendulum of a certain length would oscillate at the exact same rate, regardless of the height from which it was let go. This he concluded by measuring the time it took to swing back and forth, using his heartbeat as a guide. It was yet another message from God, which Dromo would in time decipher. But for now the drool abandoned Fleque's lip to form a glutinous puddle on his trouser leg. He wiped it away with the back of a careless hand, which action swiftly brought an end to Dromo's scientific musing.

Fleque gave a sigh, hauling himself painfully to his feet and making his way slowly to the door. Dromo could not bear to let him leave without answering the question that trembled on his lips, though he could equally not bear to hear the answer. He swallowed hard.

"Antoine... when will they come for me?"

Antoine shrugged and Dromo realised it had been foolish of him to ask it anyway. No one would tell Fleque anything.

"Little monk want leave Antoine now. Your time come soon. They want rid of you. No more you books. No more you writing."

He gestured at *Doctrina*, curling his lip at the words and symbols lying therein, as though he had taken a bite from something unexpectedly bitter. Dromo's hands clasped the edges of the ledger in an involuntary protective movement. Antoine had never shown the slightest interest in his work before, but since the king's terrifying pardon, anything now seemed possible. Fleque caught the scent of Dromo's fear and a malevolent gleam flashed across his mottled, dirt-streaked face. He moved closer, tilting his head towards the page, nodding sagely as though he could make perfect sense of the diagrams and geometrical shapes that lay there. Dromo tightened his grip. Fleque traced a finger across the page, leaving a greasy trail of sweat on the stark white parchment. He made a sudden movement to occupy the stool where Dromo presently sat, paying no attention to the fact that the little monk was pushed roughly to the floor by his bulk. And now he hunched over the book, taking its cover in his hands, staring down intently at Dromo's cherished formulae, his sacred diagrams. Dromo's heart was in his mouth. He loved Antoine but he loved *Doctrina* more. He could not bear to see it touched, and here was a brutish, indifferent man apparently about to consume it whole.

As it turned out he needn't have worried, for his gaoler had no apparent desire to upset his charge by defiling the thing that he loved most. Dromo noticed something besides contempt in Antoine's puzzled scrutiny of the graphs and diagrams. He peered closely at the page before his eyes, contemplating the most recent of Dromo's meticulously crafted illustrations, the honeycomb of interlocking hexagons. He sniffed at it, then turned to the prisoner with a crooked smile. His eyes were moist, and Dromo feared he might burst into tears once more.

"Pretty," was all he said.

---o0o---

As soon as Antoine Fleque began his unusually laboured ascent of the stone staircase Dromo knew that something was wrong. His footfall, that Dromo knew better than his own heartbeat, sounded a different note to normal. It seemed an eternity before the lumbering guard finally arrived at his cell door. When the door swung open, it was immediately clear why Fleque had struggled with the long climb. Dromo's heart sank.

The plan had formed quickly, of necessity, inspired by Fleque's sudden interest in his work. Dromo had no history of cunning, but the urgency of his predicament demanded that he take immediate action to prevent his release from ever taking place. At all costs he must not leave this cell, this sanctuary, his only home, the one place where he knew himself to be safe. If nothing else, he was close to unlocking the great secret that lay at the heart of mathematics, close to penetrating the mysterious code that he alone could decipher. Such important work could not be put aside for a moment. Witness his confusion on returning from the throne room, his inability to recall the revelation that God in His infinite wisdom had whispered to him. This alone was clear evidence that he must not be forced to leave the castle. Why, even the thought of it had begun to cloud his mind. He had no doubt that he would bring to mind the revelation, an idea so simple, so fundamental that it could not be forgotten indefinitely. This urgent matter must first be dealt with, after which he would resume his studies from exactly where he left off.

But could he put his plan into action before he met his fate? He imagined a phalanx of guards clattering up towards his lofty cell, clamouring to lay their hands upon him and offer him up to the myriad dangers of the dreaded world outside the castle walls. It could happen at any hour, at any moment. Three days had passed since the king's pardon, during which time Dromo had become acquainted with a whole new emotion, hitherto unknown to him. This, he reasoned, was what they called fear, a tightening of the sinews that began in the stomach, climbed upwards to the neck and shoulders, then finally seized upon the mind, sending it spinning like a leaf in a gale. The feeling intensified until Dromo almost began to wish the doomed exile would actually happen, if only to relieve him of the pangs of its anticipation.

He needed Antoine Fleque to be the architect of his cleverly conceived deception, which involved confessing to a crime of sufficient magnitude that it would assure him of his permanent further residency at the top of the tower. But herein lay the problem. Antoine had grown noticeably angrier these last few days, and was spending far less time in Dromo's company. It was as though he could not bear to lay eyes upon the prisoner that he had treated with such casual cruelty for so long, and like a child forced to give up its favourite plaything he had retreated into a sullen, irascible mood.

Dromo did not take offence, for he had always known that deep within the pungent breast of Antoine Fleque there beat the heart of a man more sinned against than sinning. What's more, he understood that Antoine needed him, depended upon him, and was just as desperate for Dromo to remain imprisoned as he was himself. In this light, Antoine's mood was wholly understandable. Sensing that time was running out, he felt the only way to be compensated for the loss of his prisoner was to redouble his disciplinary effort. He invented new punishments for crimes of increasing pettiness. The monk found that to so much as look out of the window was now a significant transgression of the rules. At one point, when he reached for his bowl of gruel, newly placed at his feet only moments before, Fleque kicked it across the floor before Dromo could pick it up. He then left the room, slamming the cell door behind him, turning the key in the lock with a resounding clank, as if to remind Dromo that he was still imprisoned. When he returned later it was not to replace the spilled supper but rather to accuse Dromo of having broken the bowl himself, a charge that required repayment by means of a stern admonishment followed by a prolonged bout of sulking from the admonisher.

Dromo pranced and darted hither and thither, ducking from the worst of these blows while surrendering to others, maintaining his cheerful disposition and at all times trying, but failing, to engage his beloved gaoler in conversation. His idea, in essence, was a very simple one. He would contrive to have *Doctrina* open at the page Fleque had admired, and having thus drawn his attention to the work, he would then make bold his assertion that the sun did not revolve around the earth but the other way around, that in fact the earth was not the centre of the universe but a satellite of the sun, like those wandering stars whose movement through the heavens Dromo had deduced made them satellites, too, and therefore not stars at all but objects like the earth. He knew that this fact, though proved by observation, was in contradiction of the prevailing wisdom. But those who professed the belief that the earth had been placed at the centre of all things clearly did not share the vantage point that Dromo enjoyed at the top of his tower. If they could only see what he saw, they would surely change their minds. In idle hours, during daily exercise, he had overheard men talk of these things. He had never felt the need to correct them, not wishing to incur their wrath. But now he had no choice. The only way out, or in this case the only way to remain inside, was by subtle and devious means to let Antoine Fleque know of his findings. Antoine would alert the king that a grave and serious crime had taken place at the top of the tower, punishable, Dromo felt sure, by a further lifetime's incarceration.

So far, so good, but now, when the door was flung back revealing Antoine standing there, wheezing and puffing, straining under the heavy burden that he had wrestled up the spiral stairway, Dromo realised with renewed fear that he may not have time to carry out his plan at all. Antoine staggered over to the desk and slammed the great wooden platter down on top of *Doctrina*, completely obscuring the page that the monk had left open to entice his victim with its geometric patterns and its elegant equations. Piled on the wooden board in great heaps was a magnificent feast. There were capons, gleaming and bronzed from the spit; there were grapes and figs, black dates shining like pitch, apples glinting with their sweet juices; there was wine and a flagon of ale.

Dromo knew what this all meant. This was his last supper. This meant that his time was up. Fleque panted and swore under what little breath remained to him, fixing Dromo with a murderous, accusing look, a look that foretold of dire consequences for the monk. Of all the many insults and indignities Fleque had endured, the look seemed to say, this was the worst.

"Food… for you," he croaked, his eyes bloodshot from rage and exertion. "While Antoine fed on slops, monk may eat his fill."

Fleque spat on the floor in disgust, the arc of his spittle narrowly missing a fragrant basket of bread. In the silence that followed, Dromo struggled to think of a suitable response.

"It's awfully kind, Antoine. Could you please tell cook that I am not hungry?"

This was evidently not the correct one, as Fleque gave vent to a bellow of jealous anger, shaking his head from side to side with such violence that beads of sweat sprayed from his hair in all directions. Suddenly he lunged at Dromo, scattering green olives across the stone floor. He took the little monk by the throat, hauling him off his feet in one motion. His grip tightened as Dromo hung there, feet flapping helplessly below him. Fleque's eyes were glazed over with hatred, or love, or perhaps something in between. For a moment it seemed he was about to murder Dromo there and then. The monk felt he was losing consciousness. He barely managed to splutter out the words that might save him.

"Antoine... no. Please... I have something to tell you..."

Sure enough, Antoine sagged, letting Dromo slip to the floor. He leaned his oversized head against the wall for a moment, as though to cool his brow on the rough stones. Then he, too, slumped down, so that gaoler and prisoner sat next to each other, backs against the wall. There they remained in silence for some time, Antoine staring ahead at nothing in particular, lost and alone. Then at last Dromo spoke up without rancour, his enthusiasm as boundless as ever.

"Antoine.... I must tell you. I have been watching the stars for some time now, and I find I simply must confide in somebody."

Antoine did not respond, but Dromo continued as though he had professed the greatest interest.

"Yes. It would seem that I have made the most wondrous discovery, to do with the very earth on which we stand."

---oOo---

For several hours, despite the feelings of dread that gripped him, Dromo had tried to work. The weather outside his window had grown noticeably cooler, purple clouds pressing in on the castle walls, trees far below bending to the stiff autumnal breeze, releasing their leaves as he, Dromo, would soon be released. Like the leaves he would surely fall and be damned if his plan did not work.

At first, after Antoine left, he had tried to get back to *Doctrina*, tried with an increasing edge of desperation to cast his mind back to the throne room and those precious moments before the king had pardoned him, the last moments during which his mind had been free of this grinding doubt and fear. How he wished to return to that innocent time. Was it gone for good? But no, it couldn't be. He knew that it was within his power to recall the message that God, in His infinite wisdom, had conveyed to him, using the hexagons as His divine messengers. The revelation had been so clear, and so simple. It would come to him, he felt sure, but not yet, not now. His plan was all.

Mostly he was exhausted from the trial that had been his long, slow attempt to educate Antoine Fleque in God's heavenly dance of the spheres. For the best part of the afternoon, as tendrils of mist crept over the walls of his lofty home like ivy, Dromo had described the motion of the planets in their orbit around the sun to his audience of one. By the use of analogy, and by tracing with a finger on cold stone slabs the arc of the moon as it spun around its earthly host, now illuminated by the sun, now half-buried in endless, unfathomable night, he gave a lesson on the effects of these vast celestial bodies, one upon the other. The planets, Dromo had deduced, lay on a vast plane, placed, as it were, upon a dish of enormous size, some near to the centre, others very much further away at the rim. As they revolved about the sun they did so in regular and discrete orbits that only seemed to us to have a random element because of our unique perspective, being bound to the earth that both spins about its axis, giving us the day and the night, and orbits the sun, giving us the seasons.

In truth you would be hard-pressed to know for sure whether Antoine Fleque had properly received this instruction, for although he had given out the occasional grunt in reply to Dromo's questioning endearments - "Have you understood me, Antoine?" "Would you care for me to repeat that last bit, Antoine?" - he never once spoke throughout the lesson, his mouth being full at all times with the meal that had been intended for Dromo. With a focused deliberation that was as grotesque as it was indelicate, Fleque had mauled at the food like a half-starved wolf, tearing at chunks of meat with blackened fingers, slurping at gravy, much of which missed his slavering mouth, spilled down his chin and disappeared into the dark undergrowth of his thick, black chest hair, dismembering the capons by rolling their carcasses around in his maw, then spitting out their bones like a regurgitating hawk. Washing every mouthful down with great, gargled drafts of ale, he would occasionally rend the air with cavernous belches. At one point, when Dromo had been using an apple to demonstrate the way in which the earth was tilted at an angle to the celestial plane, Fleque had responded by grabbing it from his tutor, giving it a quizzical look, then devouring it in three noisy bites, core and all.

Nevertheless, he had submitted to the lesson. Afterwards, when every last scrap of food had been consumed, leaving only a crust of bread soaking up a pool of grease on the cell floor, Fleque had hauled himself up like a wounded bear and left, locking the door behind him, to sleep off the feast in whatever dark underground recess of the castle he was accustomed to lay his filthy head. Dromo was equally spent, but found he could not rest. He wondered how much of the lesson had been truly absorbed. For it was to be hoped that Antoine would be spurred into action by the last thing Dromo had said before his gaoler left, the high point of the monk's devious plan: "Please remember, Antoine, you must not alert the king's advisors to my findings, which are quite blasphemous. Were you to do so, it could mean this sentence of mine, now repealed, might yet be reinstated, and its length even redoubled!"

Unable to further concentrate on scientific matters, Dromo did what he always did when the mood took him, usually on cloudy days when God's wondrous gifts were not readily available to him: he hefted *Doctrina* back into its place in the alcove where it rested next to its twin, *Fabula,* an identical leather-bound tome. These two books were his treasures: *Doctrina* always on the left, *Fabula* on the right.

This second book he had reserved for writing his many and various accounts of the lives of his near neighbours in the town of Boroglass, stories he was obliged to conjure for himself, being unable to see beyond the rooftops of their dwellings. From the glimpses he was afforded of the townsfolk going about their business he was able to invent all manner of human interactions, weddings and funerals, merry meetings and bitter disputes, writing as the fancy took him, with little care for narrative cohesion. Now with some little effort he took the book down and carefully carried it to his desk. The pages fell open at his last entry, which he now read over, finding in the repetition of the words a soothing balm for his troubled soul.

One of the joyful aspects of this second book was the way in which it allowed his mind to wander freely, just like his made-up heroes and villains, from one adventure to the next. This was in stark contrast to *Doctrina*, where calculation and strict adherence to logical axioms guided Dromo, inch by inch, towards the unveiling of a universal truth. *Fabula* called for an opposite approach. In storytelling truth emerged, as it were, by accident, if it emerged at all, with events and images tumbling over one another seemingly at random, so that sometimes he fancied it was his quill pen that was doing the work, while he himself looked on in amused detachment. Having reached a high point in one story, Dromo was ever keen to discover what would happen next to his fictional counterparts. But further enlightenment would have to wait as sleep's beckoning became more urgent. His quill slipped from his hand before he could write a word, and he was quickly overcome. He slumped forward on the desk. His eyes closed, and when he eventually opened them, it was morning.

---oOo---

He came to consciousness by degrees, woken by a pain in his skull that rang with the force of hammer blows. For a few moments he fought to remember what he had been doing the previous night. Then slowly, painfully, the memory of his deception of poor Antoine Fleque returned. His first impulse was to curse himself for the way he had so duped his poor, innocent friend. Antoine did not deserve such treatment, for all his faults. Antoine had never known kindness, and did not trust it when he encountered it. But Dromo still loved him, and with that realisation he told himself that what he had done was for their mutual benefit. The goal was to maintain their friendship, after all, not destroy it.

Something was missing, he quickly realised. He rose to his feet and lurched across his cell towards the empty stone ledge, fumbling with trembling hands along it like a blind man. All was lost. He spun on his heels with a helpless, guttural cry. No point in searching about him, for there was nowhere to look, no corners in which the books could have been hidden. His books, his two books! His life's work was gone.

Dromo threw himself at his cell door in a panic.

"Antoine! Antoine, for pity's sake!"

He attacked the great wooden door with his fists until they began to bleed, all the while babbling and calling his gaoler's name. Then gradually he realised that the pounding that sounded so like hammers was not in his head but outside, somewhere below. He sprang across to the window with all the speed that his stout legs could muster, bringing his wooden stool after him. Climbing up, he hauled his body into a position from which he could view the battlements, just as the pounding ceased.

The cloying mist that had enveloped the castle the previous night had dispelled, but oh, how Dromo wished it would return to spare his eyes from the sight that greeted them! There below he saw that what had been constructed, hammer blow by hammer blow, was a crude wooden gallows. There were people gathered there. Something momentous was evidently about to happen, and the dangling noose left no doubt as to what that might be. After a while King Ludovico appeared and stood to one side of the gallows, in full regalia, orating to the crowd with sweeping, expansive gestures. Fragments of his words drifted up to Dromo's perch but they were distorted, carried off by the wind before he could decipher them. Dromo could make out faces. There were knights with their squires, clerics, holy men and foot soldiers, serving wenches, the high- and low-born. Many more, he guessed, were out of his sight line, no matter how he stretched. Perhaps the entire population of the castle had been assembled, save the prisoners.

At first he did not notice the smoke. It was not exceptional for a fire to be lit along the battlements and ramparts of the castle, to clear away dead leaves, or to send a signal, or simply to provide warmth for whoever was on duty there. This one, set in an iron brazier, was large, with orange flames that waved and gusted frantically in the frosty air. There was no thought in Dromo's mind to their composition, no time for questions. He saw not God's handiwork this time but instead an angry blaze, and surrounding it an angry throng.

At last the king finished speaking and gestured for a lackey to bring something forth. Dromo held his breath as he caught sight of what was to be sacrificed. One of his books – it had to be *Doctrina*, was presented to the crowd who immediately voiced their contempt. Even from here Dromo could see their gargoyle features, twisted with hate, fists clenched to scorn the Devil. The book was raised up and when the crowd's angry chanting finally abated, the king's men ritually fed it to the flames. A cheer went up.

Then, to Dromo's mounting horror, the condemned man was brought forth. The king made a further short speech, and the next sounds to reach Dromo's ears were the worst of all. Antoine Fleque protested his innocence with a series of pitiable cries that cut through the monk's ribs like a steel blade and pierced his heart.

It happened swiftly, while Dromo tried with all his might to look away but found he could not. Perhaps he owed it to his hapless gaoler to stand witness. Antoine was led, still protesting, up the wooden steps. A blindfold was wrapped about his eyes, and instantly the trapdoor fell away beneath him. Even the crowd held their breath now. There was the briefest of struggles then all was quiet.

---oOo---

It was market day in the village of San Gemini, nestled at the entrance to a wooded valley draped in its russet and purple cloak that shone like burnished copper in the haze of midday. A ragged, stick-like figure descended from a copse of trees and made his way slowly across a great expanse of green pasture. This was the fairest season of them all, thought Palini. Before rain clouds, sleet and snow drained all colour from land and sky, while autumn leaves still proudly declaimed their presence with their bold display, nature herself seemed to be taking stock. It was not a new beginning but a glorious and optimistic ending. The pale sun hadn't lost its power to warm his bones. The air was crisp and clean, cooling him even as it warmed him. Bring on the winter, he thought to himself, it holds no fear for me.

Palini wanted sustenance, and he was going to find it. He had never questioned where his food came from before. He had merely offered up a prayer and it would come to him. Not always in the form he would have wished, and not always when he needed it most desperately, but it would come. He had always trusted that God meant him to be poor, that this was part of His plan, and that all would be revealed to him in the life to come. His place in Heaven was assured, he knew, so long as he held to this one truth.

He had known happiness in his life, along with the misery and hardship. His wretched empty belly aside, there had always been pleasure to be taken in the simplest things, in contemplation of the beauty of a flower, the sweet innocence of a child, the softness of a maiden's cheek. Though his beloved Margery had been taken from him, still he could gain some comfort from the memory of her touch. Meanwhile work would occupy his restless mind. Even harsh labour and toil had its compensations for a man. Stripped to the waist beneath an unforgiving sun, heaving an axe, straining to lift a bale of hay onto a cart, these things offered their own comforts, their own rewards. There was a certain reassurance to wanting, and having, nothing. It calmed him. He would wait, and he would pray, and he would try to see his life as an unfolding gift, as the preachers would have it in their sermons.

But always the hunger would return. And since his chance meeting with the Duc de Pomerance and their late-night musings on fate and free will, the thought had taken root in Palini's mind that there might be another way to live, one in which he took a more active role. So it was with a new sense of purpose that he strode into the marketplace of the bustling village, looked around him and considered his options. It was his custom on entering a town or hamlet where he wasn't known to lie low for a while, biding his time until an opportunity to ask for work arose. Those who needed help with shoeing a horse or mending a fence, stacking some barrels or rounding up a pig for slaughter would, if he was lucky, sense his humble presence and with a wordless nod direct him to the task at hand. When it was completed there would be some scraps of food, perhaps a little beer or wine, rarely a conversation, rarer still a proffered 'thank you'.

There were people trading in every corner, and the air was filled with the clamour of their boastful exhortations. The wares on offer included scrawny goats and a few cows, chickens crammed into wooden cages, their farmyard squabbles adding to the general hubbub. There were barrels of olives, honeycombs, rounded heaps of walnuts and great rounds of cheese. A few poor urchins scampered here and there, hoping to outrun the dogs if an apple or perhaps a peach was to fall from one of the carts.

It was a familiar enough scene, but today Palini sensed something was different. It took him a little while to realise just how many eyes were upon him as he wandered from stall to stall. He was unused to seeing folk look in his direction, or acknowledge him in any way, for poverty will make a man invisible to his fellows, so sought an explanation. Palini truly felt himself to be transformed, reborn, from this one chance encounter with a man of substance, a man who sought his own destiny, the Duc de Pomerance. Could it be that others recognised the change in him, at a single glance? No, this was too much to expect. It was his height that had intrigued them, he told himself, as he ducked under the wooden sill of a narrow doorway, lured by the smell of hops and malt.

It was cool in the inn, a place of shadows and dark oak recesses that drew him deeper inside, so that the hum of the market traders gradually died away. Small groups of men sat in corners, nursing their tankards and murmuring together in conspiratorial huddles. A serving wench approached Palini with a suspicious look that he answered with the broadest grin. He ordered boiled ham, bread and figs. When he reached into his pocket and slapped a coin down on the table, she returned his smile with a shy grin of her own and took the coin, which swiftly disappeared into her cleavage. When the food arrived, an unctuous and fatty cut of meat still smoking from the pot and glazed with honey, he ate hungrily, feeling like a king. The wench brought water in a jug, so that after each succulent mouthful of meat and bread he could wash his palate clean. Hunger sated, he slowed his pace to nibble contentedly at chunks of fresh fig then finally sat back with a sigh of pleasure, thinking back over the events of the last twelve hours.

It hadn't been his plan to steal from Edouard Apery. He had genuinely tried to sleep but felt so haunted by the Duc's words that he could not manage it. Instead he found himself remembering past moments of his life, reviewing the decisions he had made in the light of his new knowledge. Had he not spoken to the Duc de Pomerance and shared his supper with him, had he merely heard about the rich man's philosophy from some second-hand source, he would surely have accused him of committing the sin of blasphemy. But here was the point that he returned to in his mind, again and again. Edouard had not denied God's universal laws. He had merely reinterpreted them. It was surely no coincidence, given the immensity of the woodland he had been adrift in for the last month, that he should meet the Duc in the way he did. Our destiny being mapped out for us at every point, this was a clear message from God to one of His most humble servants. And when the Duc's purse had slipped from his belt as he slumbered, almost rolling into the ashes of the fire, Palini had seen this as another sign. He had reached down for the purse, intending to reattach it to the Duc's belt. Before he could, however, the purse dislodged two coins onto the ground at his feet.

He did not covet others' wealth, he did not seek riches, nor to achieve status for himself that was not deserved. He sought only to know his true path, as God had ordained it, and to fill his belly. But these two goals had often seemed at odds with one another. Perhaps, as the Duc had suggested, his fault had been to wait, and not to act. The old Palini would have slipped those two coins back into the purse, quietly so as not to wake their owner. Would this have been the correct choice, the one sanctioned by the all-seeing, all-powerful God who presided over his thoughts and deeds? Or would that same God have chided him, have scorned him for seeing the message and not acting upon it? Two messages were hard to ignore, the first from the lips of Edouard Apery, willing Palini to make choices, the second in the form of these coins. Was he to ignore them both?

The Duc de Pomerance was a rich man. The purse had been heavy with coins, and Palini had been modest in his decision to take only two. Their owner would not miss them. If he did, Palini reassured himself, the Duc would merely smile to know that his lesson on free will had been well received, that his pupil had exercised that very same free will to levy payment for the fish that had been so gratefully consumed, one favour for another.

Palini yawned and stretched. It was customary in such an establishment for one to stay the night before moving on. There would be a straw bed and a blanket for a weary traveller, and perhaps a mug of wine or mead. In the morning he could expect a fresh egg or two and a drink of water for the road ahead. The coin he had given the serving wench would more than cover these provisions. But it was too early to think of such things, and he did not relish the thought of moving on right away, or seeking employment elsewhere in the village, as he would have done in the past. He wanted to sit and ruminate on his life, to compare and contrast the old Palini, his marriage, the death of his wife and the birth of his son, and the subsequent events that had led him to wander the world, with this new, invigorated, purposeful Palini who made choices and took control of things. More than this, he wanted to reward himself for his ingenuity and spirit.

The oak bench seemed to shape its contours to his bony body. All weariness was banished. He felt embraced by the inn and its warm shadows. The men who huddled in corners seemed less threatening to him somehow. One of them looked over, raising a glass in greeting, and Palini smiled back. Calling the wench over, he ordered wine for himself and his fellows. He reached into his pocket and produced the second coin as payment. The serving girl smiled prettily, looking to the wanderer even fairer than she had before.

---oOo---

The prayers had continued long into the night, ushering the baby along on his journey, willing him to let go, but Palini's newborn son, scarcely bigger than Palini's fist, refused to die. The skin on his tiny body looked ill-fitting and ancient. It was mottled with purple patches so that he resembled a skinned rabbit. His mouth hung open, for he had not the strength in his jaw to close it. This, along with his skinny, helpless limbs made him look more like a tiny, wizened old man at the end of his life than a baby at his very beginning. Some of the women who had gathered were muttering about a miracle. Others thought it was unnatural and a bad omen to keep this odd-looking creature alive. Custom told them that he should be respectfully disposed of, along with his twin. Not in any cruel way of course, the baby would simply not be fed, and after a little while he would pass into the next world from malnutrition. Born as he was before the allotted nine moons had passed, it was argued that his life had not been willed by the Almighty. For Palini, still in shock at the loss of his dearest Margery, neither choice made any sense. He was quite incapable of feeling or speech as he sat by the corpse of his wife, silently begging her forgiveness, quite certain that this tragic turn of events was his fault. In the event the decision was made for him by a young woman who had recently been delivered of a child and who came forward offering to suckle the tiny lad.

By degrees, and after many fraught moments when it seemed the boy had indeed breathed his last, he grew stronger, learning to suck at his benefactor's teat and even looking about him, though it would be many months before he could form sounds or let out a cry. None of this was a source of comfort for Palini, who had neither the will nor the inclination to raise a child alone. What skills could he bring to bear, a poor woodcutter and helping hand? This boy was every bit as much a punishment for unnamed sins as was the death of his wife, perhaps more so, since he could not abandon a child with good conscience. It was evidently God's will that he had been left this legacy and he was determined to accept and bring up his son, or to try at least, however difficult the task.

Palini and his wife had been residing with the miller. Jon was a gruff and silent man who nevertheless was smitten with his grandson from the start, translating into love for the child his grief at the passing of his daughter. So it was that in the early stages of the boy's development it was his grandfather who nurtured him while Palini took a more active role in the family business, toiling daily in the small bakery by the millstream. It was his grandfather too who had named him, along with his brother, for Jon insisted that the dead twin have an equal right to existence, if not in this world then the next. So the surviving twin became Matthew, and his brother in Heaven was Luke.

Palini lost himself in his daily, and nightly, routines. In company with all bakers everywhere he gradually took on the appearance of a ghost, exhausted from the long hours and never without a liberal dusting of flour from his boots to his eyelashes. He worked to rid himself of the guilt he felt in his heart, a guilt that he shared with no man. Sometimes at the end of a long day Jon would try to prise from him this terrible secret as they shared their evening meal. But the younger man could scarcely be coaxed from his brooding silence or dissuaded from his conviction that he had strayed somehow. Not in deed perhaps but in thought, and this was the result, a lifetime of penance. His former dalliances with the fairer sex were forgotten. He was a widower for whom even the thought of human contact brought doubt and shame. Sensing the change in him the local maidens soon learned to pass by his stall, or if they did stop to purchase bread they would do so wordlessly, bowing their heads as they handed over their money, then moving off swiftly without a backward glance.

Matthew, despite his inauspicious entry into the world, grew quickly. He was, after all, grandson to a baker. Whatever Palini's faults as a parent, he was a good provider, bartering his coarsely milled flour and other wares for the odd chicken or fish, pulses and fruits, even a suckling pig at feast times, and the boy's appetite was an equal match for all. With the emergence of his teeth he ate as though to make up time, and by the eighth or ninth year of his life he was shouldering bags of flour almost equal to his own weight. Useful as he was to the business, Matthew and Palini could not get along. The trauma of his birth still hung over his father, clouding his reason, but the main point of contention was not Palini's surviving son, but the one who had died.

Luke had been gathered to his maker's bosom before the taint of human weakness had attached itself to him. By virtue of his death, he was sanctified and pure, beyond all suffering and beyond the earthly realm where his brother now resided. So it was that if ever the growing boy transgressed in his father's eyes, which being young he regularly did, Palini would evoke the spirit of the dead child, and draw inevitable comparisons. Luke would never soil a bag of flour in some unfortunate, incontinent episode, nor upturn a batch of fresh loaves into the mud, however accidentally. And Luke did not cry at night, disturbing his poor father's precious few hours of rest. Many a time Palini found he had to rouse himself at the cock's crow scant minutes after his body had gratefully succumbed to the gift of sleep, and he found it hard in the extreme not to blame the boy.

From day to day, and year to year, an evocation of the spirit of Luke was never far from Palini's lips. Matthew, in common with all children knowing no better, understood himself to be fairly, if harshly, judged. He strove to be worthy of his dead brother, but nevertheless over time grew resentful of Luke, whose continuing presence, albeit in the afterlife, served as proof and validation of his own wretched inadequacy. He loved his father, but rarely did he manage by his own actions to break through the cloud of despondency that permanently hung about Palini. The only saving grace for Matthew was his grandfather. Jon doted on the child, but he was an old man in failing health, and when at last his frail, dust-choked lungs breathed their last, a vital link in Matthew's young life was eternally severed.

They buried the old man by the millstream next to Margery, father and daughter reunited at last, after which Palini the baker and his son were left alone.

Palini had aged rapidly in the few years since his marriage. His facial features, once aquiline and well defined now had sunk deeper into his skull, giving him the appearance of a cadaver. The hooded, sleepless eyes orbited their bony sockets, rarely meeting another's gaze except to greet a customer or a supplier. Even his gait betrayed his underlying sadness. He became a little stooped, and his joints cracked like dry twigs when he walked. Matthew, on the verge of manhood, was the opposite in physical character, having been blessed with his mother's more robust frame. The heavy workload, moving from farm to mill to bakery and back again, had broadened his back and hardened his muscular physique. By his thirteenth year he was already a match for any farmhand or passing ruffian who tried to steal from the bakery or otherwise disturb the peace of the nearby village. Local folk knew that they could count on him to intervene in the event of a skirmish or raid from any warring faction that happened along, while others feared his quick temper and even quicker hands that would ball into fists as hard as ploughshares at the slightest provocation.

Yoked as both father and son were to the stresses of their life together, a day of reckoning was inevitable. When it came it was sooner than expected, and the spark that lay waste to their relationship, that blazed and burned and blackened their hearts was a tiny one. A chance remark by Palini on the subject of his lost son brought a swift rebuke from the angry youth who had once shared a womb with Luke. The pity of it was that the observation for once had not been directed at Matthew. Palini had been looking at a sunset, and in a rare moment of tranquillity, had expressed the wish that Luke could have been there to enjoy it with him. Matthew snapped back at his father, which in turn angered Palini. How was it that his surviving son, with all the advantages of a beating heart, with eyes that could see and limbs that could move, possessed none of the angelic qualities of his brother who had been denied these gifts? Perhaps, then, countered Matthew, Palini had rather Luke had lived than he. When this met with no reply, the boy who was almost a man took stock. In a broken voice he swore that these eyes he had been granted, incidentally now misted over with tears, had seen all they wanted to see, and that these limbs he had been granted could indeed move. He left the bakery that night, never to return.

---oOo---

He had been drinking all day since his meal of boiled ham and figs. Now Palini was in his cups, and quite in his element. It was gone midnight and he had taken to regaling the assembled company with the story of his meeting with the Duc and their frank discussion about free will, for good measure leaving out the part where he had robbed him of some money. All this while the inn had been gradually filling with rough men of some unspecified regiment. Each was arraigned in battledress of a similar dull hue, and all wore weapons at their belts, axes, swords and maces. Similar such weapons had evidently been used on them, too, judging by the deep scars on their faces that ran from ear to ear, disappeared into their beards or crossed their foreheads and cheeks like cracks in a dry riverbed.

Palini had been too preoccupied with his newfound status as an accomplished storyteller to take much notice of this development, especially since the fellows at his table had been so generous towards him, refilling his tankard when necessary and raucously laughing or indeed gasping at even the most uninspiring of his adventures. But now he became aware of a generalised note of tension as the beer flowed and the men's tongues loosened around him. Evidently this was no harvest festival or feast day celebration but another, altogether darker ritual gathering. It seemed there would be a battle the next morning, and these warriors were engaged in animated tactical debate, agitating with each other, stirring each other's bloodlust in preparation for the coming carnage. Fortunately for Palini he was not so drunk that he did not recognise the potential danger of his situation, and this realisation had a sudden and profoundly sobering effect on him. Everywhere he looked there were groups of men, four or five in number, gesticulating with fierce expressions, demonstrating how they would sever this man's ears, that one's limbs, club or stab or otherwise eviscerate a third.

There were two, and only two, savage, warring tribes in this region: the Mendicans and the Szarks. Over many decades, if not centuries, they had vied for territory in a succession of wars each bloodier than the last, creating in the process a flourishing trade for map-makers who were repeatedly obliged to draw and redraw the boundary between the two nations to reflect each new conquest. The Mendicans were a fiercely proud, combative race who spent their days either waging war or rehearsing for it through the many bloodthirsty games which their king, Gustav, had modelled for them after the gladiators of antiquity. The same could not be said about the Szarks who were at least outwardly more genteel, enjoying the finer arts of poetry, pottery and silk weaving. But the Szarks had a reputation for duplicity and cunning. When it came to dealing with their enemies they put aside the finer things and transformed themselves into rioting, rampaging beasts of prey.

As he looked cautiously around, so as not to draw attention to himself, it dawned on Palini that he could not tell which of the two tribes these men belonged to, and this thought began to trouble him greatly. Despite the angry roaring of voices that was beginning to resound throughout the inn, it was becoming impossible to distinguish individual words. For a moment Palini sighed with relief when he heard the word 'Mendican' uttered with force. This could only mean the men were Szarks, planning a raid on their enemy. But then, as though on cue, he heard the word 'Szark' from another quarter, voiced with equal venom, so that the whole question of their identity was again thrown into doubt.

Almost at the same instant Palini noticed that one of his immediate neighbours, a man who had introduced himself as Pietro de Fey, was scrutinising him closely. Pietro had been one of the most enthusiastic members of his small audience, and had actually wept with laughter at one of the misadventures Palini had told of, but now his expression had taken on a quizzical nature. Palini broke into a sweat, wondering how he could quickly extricate himself from the proceedings, but before he could move to do so, he was held fast by Pietro's hand on his arm.

"Are you alright, Palini?" he asked with a friendly smile.

"Oh yes … quite alright." Palini hoped the catch in his voice would pass for evidence of drunkenness rather than fear. He ran a damp hand across his forehead.

"It is a little late. And I am hot. Perhaps I have a fever."

Pietro took no notice of the complaint but suddenly changed tack, further unnerving Palini.

"You do not seem prepared for battle. Have you even signed the pledge? We will be engaging with the enemy at daybreak."

"An oversight. I will take the pledge here and now if you direct me to the commanding officer. Where are they camped… the enemy?"

Palini was floundering, hoping by a show of enthusiasm that he could buy himself some time. Surely Pietro would let slip the name of the tribe they were soon to be fighting. Then again, judging by the way he was studying him askance, it was quite possible that he had guessed Palini's predicament and was purposefully leading him on to expose himself as one of the enemy himself and thus fodder for the sharpened, deadly instruments of warfare hanging from the belts all around them.

Palini knew that to plead neutrality was hopeless. Mendicans and Szarks alike detested outsiders, looking upon vagrants as they would stray dogs, and disposing of them with equal sangfroid. Such men as scorned the fight would be shown less mercy than would a member of the hated other camp. Nor would they make allowances for his age. There were as many grey beards among the assembly as black. Palini's only chance lay in declaring himself, here and now, a Mendican or a Szark. But if he got it wrong it would mean certain death. And as he held Pietro's gaze, too afraid to look away, he knew with absolute certainty that he had been led to this point, for others around the table were also studying him with suspicious eyes. Then Pietro answered his question with a pointed question of his own.

"The enemy? What enemy? Do you mean Szark or Mendican?" Another smile, thinner this time, more knowing.

Palini was undone. All those stories he had so foolishly recounted now resounded in his mind, which, despite his considerable consumption of wine, was suddenly and alarmingly clear. Mendican or Szark, Szark or Mendican? Was this another divine test, another chance to see what the new Palini could do that the old would shy away from? He would make a bold claim here and now. He would say to Pietro, loudly and defiantly, that he was a Mendican, and take the consequences.

The more he turned this idea over in his head, the more convinced of it he became. And Mendicans, he knew, had a great love of blunt weapons, where Szarks preferred the short sword. Everywhere he looked he saw maces. These were Mendicans, there could be no doubt about it. His mind raced back to the two coins that had fallen from the Duc's purse. A choice had been presented to him, to take the coins or to leave them, and he had gone with his first instinct. Now instinct was leading him once more. God did not figure in this decision, merely providing the choice. It was up to Palini now. The words that would release or condemn him were on his lips. But just as he was about to utter them a scuffle broke out between a couple of the foot soldiers, apparently in disagreement about the correct use of a claymore. The noise in the room increased as others sought to quell the violence, or in some cases add to it, but Palini could not take his eyes off his silent accuser, Pietro de Fey.

Suddenly the choice he was about to make seemed to offer less hope than before, so he abruptly changed tack and without a conscious thought in his head suddenly bounded up from the bench and leaped onto the solid oak table, letting out a bold shout, bringing everyone to order.

The room fell silent as all eyes were turned towards him. A great mass of sweating, ugly male flesh glared in his direction. He barely knew what he was doing, but the die had been cast, and he glared back at the throng with all the venom and righteous disdain that he could muster. Fixing every man with a sweeping gaze, he lowered his voice to a whisper, so that even the proudest warrior was forced to lean towards him.

"Save your strength for the battle, my brothers. While we make merry with these … entertainments, the enemy sleeps soundly, harnessing his strength." Palini allowed his voice to gain in volume and momentum. "Your fury is misplaced. The enemy would laugh to see you spend it on each other. He who agrees say Aye."

"Aye!" said one warrior who, finding himself a lone voice, glanced nervously at his fellows. Palini was merciless. He would convert the whole room to his aims or die in the attempt.

"Well?" he shouted. "Will we win the day?"

"Aye!" More joined the chorus this time, nodding their heads, daring each other to disagree. The tide was turning, but the day was not yet won. Palini had seized the initiative and could sense that he was almost free. He looked defiantly down at Pietro, who was wide-eyed with something like admiration. In the brief exchange of glances that passed between them, there was a hint of recognition. It would take just one more effort, one more push. He looked back at the crowd.

"Let me hear your battle cry!" he bellowed.

"DEATH TO THE MENDICANS," came the immediate reply.

With a jubilant roar, the men thronged about Palini. Strong arms wrestled him from the table top. He barely had time to exchange a grin with Pietro de Fey before he was carried shoulder-high from the room by the Szark warriors.

3
DECEMBER

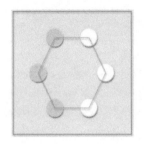

"Come closer. Let me look at you."

Dromo had been summoned for a second audience with his sovereign. This time, however, when he noticed the hexagonal pattern of grey slate tiles on which he walked, it was only in passing. He wondered what they could have meant to him before. There had been a revelation, he seemed to recall, an important one, but it had vanished from memory like dew before the rising sun. On his previous visit, his eyes had been firmly fixed, transfixed would be more appropriate, by the repeating pattern of those floor tiles. Now, looking up, he realised that there was another hexagon high above the throne. This was a large and imposing iron affair, bolted together and hung about with chains. It was tied to a rope as thick as a man's arm that was engaged in a pulley system, taking it over the heavy wooden beams supporting the throne room's vaulted ceiling to a great ring set in the far wall. The sides of the hexagon supported dozens of candles that bathed the room in a soft, orange glow. Dromo realised for the first time that the throne room had no windows. Without those candles they would be in darkness.

Dromo shuffled forward, a somewhat pitiful sight in his grubby monk's habit. He longed to be taken back to his cell where the light and the sun and the rain streamed in, where you could see for miles around, where you could think. But would he be allowed back there? And if he were to be allowed back, who would accompany him? His beloved Antoine was no more. Then again what would he do there, without his two books? How would he occupy his time?

"I said that we would let you go."

Ludovico's gaze was penetrating. On Dromo's earlier visit he had seemed bored and distracted. Now it seemed there was something on his mind.

"Unfortunately there have been some … developments. You understand that war is imminent?"

Dromo nodded respectfully, having actually no idea that war was imminent, nor really what the word meant. It was inconceivable to him that men should make war, even to the point of taking each other's lives, when God in His infinite wisdom had filled the world with so many wonders to be marvelled at.

"There are many complex issues to be weighed, and you have been walled up in the tower for a long time, little monk. Your crimes must have been great indeed. Perhaps you should have lost your life along with your liberty."

Ludovico gave a dry chuckle at the thought, raising a conspiratorial eyebrow to indicate that they were simply two rogues enjoying a joke together. Dromo's gloomy expression did not change. The king gave a sigh and settled back onto his throne. He began a long and detailed explanation of the history of his kingdom and the various threats from hostile factions that had plagued his reign. As he spoke he gestured towards the oak-lined walls, pointing out with undisguised pride and pomp this or that relic from a previous encounter with the enemy, dating back to his father, the first Ludovico, and beyond to a time when Boroglass and the surrounding area was home only to squirrels, field mice and herds of deer, before any human had staked a claim to the land.

None of it made any sense to Dromo, politics and war being so clearly contrary to God's will, but then Ludovico steered his lecture to the real message of the day, the real reason for the monk's presence in this exalted inner chamber, and now Dromo's ears pricked up.

"So you see why it's imperative that we need every one of our number to bend to the task. I fear the Mendicans and Szarks may turn against us here in Metagoria, when they have grown weary of fighting each other. In that event your skills as a scribe will be invaluable to us, Dromo. I'm afraid we cannot let you leave."

Dromo could barely take it in. Tears sprang spontaneously to his eyes and Ludovico's heart melted a little at the sight.

"You mustn't upset yourself. We will try our best to make you comfortable. There will be … privileges. Yes…." The king waved a regal hand in the air. He could not call to mind any privileges that might apply in this case. He was used to granting favours only to his knights. He could not envisage the little monk on horseback engaged in the murderous pursuit of wild animals.

"There will be … pudding," he ventured.

The prisoner continued to cry softly. So he was to return to his cell after all. And it was even hinted that he might continue to write. His heart was fit to burst with gratitude for the king's kindness, but he was also in a terrible quandary. His only privilege, the books, had been cruelly taken from him, and he dared not ask for their return. One, of course, could never be returned. That, he supposed, was *Doctrina*, and he mourned it with his very soul. But what of the other book? Had *Fabula* suffered the same fate as its twin?

Dromo had pondered deeply on the mysterious events that led to Antoine's execution. At first he had been too traumatised by the sight of his poor gaoler hanging there while the gathered throng, having witnessed his demise, merrily disbursed. His plan had been for Antoine to reveal the crime of blasphemy to the king. With luck his punishment would be a permanent incarceration. He knew of the anger that his observations of the movements of the planets would inspire. He knew there was a chance that his work, the star charts he had laboured over so meticulously, the mathematical formulae he had conceived with such loving care, would be forfeit. And so when the flames had so greedily devoured *Doctrina* he had felt a terrible pang of loss, as though a part of his own body was being torn from him. He was prepared for this. Perhaps he could begin again. But then poor Antoine Fleque, another human like him, and a beautiful soul in a twisted body, had been led out, weeping and protesting. What could it mean?

It was terrible, and it was all Dromo's fault. Antoine had merely been the messenger. He had schooled him with just enough knowledge to convey the message. Could the poor devil have accidentally given the impression that the calculations were his own? It did not seem possible that such an error could have occurred, but what other explanation could there be? There was certainly no consolation in the thought that had Antoine told the truth then he, Dromo, would have ended up dangling in the noose. He would rather have been sacrificed than see his friend suffer, even if Antoine had brought that suffering upon himself.

Part of him wanted to confess all to the king. But what purpose would it serve? It would not bring Antoine Fleque back to his cell. What's more, it could make the king appear foolish, something one must never do to a person of royal blood. After all, what course of action could the king take? Admit there had been an error, try Dromo for the crime and stage another execution? No, it was better to say nothing.

Ludovico's patience with Dromo was beginning to wane as the little monk continued to sob quietly. The countenance that had been so forgiving and kind turned a little sour.

"We will speak further, when I will let you know what services you may render me."

---oOo---

Dromo had allowed himself to be led away like a child. He was numb to the familiar sounds and smells of the castle as the guards marched him back through the endless, dimly lit corridors, past the kitchens and the servants' quarters to the base of the spiral staircase that led to his sanctuary. He climbed slowly upwards, his heart sinking with each step. As the key turned in the lock behind him, he gave a wilting sigh of relief and sank to the floor, feeling for the cool flagstones as though to embrace them. Emotion now overwhelmed him and he gave vent to a howl of anguish mixed with relief. He crouched, in an attitude somewhere between prayer and supplication, for what seemed like an age.

After a while he calmed himself and took his usual place at the window. Here was his consolation, here his respite. Here was where he had spent hour after hour in various states of rapture, engrossed by the evolution of a sunset, by the majesty of a rainbow, by the glory of the constellations wheeling about the night sky. But there was nothing of interest to see now, recent gales had denuded every tree and everywhere the ground had been turned to grey mud, churned up by carts and liberally spattered with the manure of a thousand horses. Townsfolk ducked into doorways to escape the cold winds, shielding themselves with their topcoats pulled around their ears. Dromo cared not one jot for their comings and goings, and even if he had, there was no *Fabula* in which to record them.

On the castle ramparts the gallows had been dismantled. Nothing remained to suggest that Antoine Fleque had ever swung there, life in the chill winter breeze. There had been no words spoken for him, save those that condemned him. He had known not one gram of kindness in his life. Dromo wondered about Antoine's mother. What had happened to her? What about Dromo's own mother? He could not bring her to mind. There was so much about life that he did not understand. Until this moment these things had never troubled him. His two books had filled every waking moment. But they were gone, and now his thoughts, instead of turning outwards to the world that God made, turned inwards. Who was Dromo? Who was Antoine Fleque? Who was King Ludovico? Why had they shared this castle together for so long? And what would happen to them in the future? Then he heard a strange noise, followed by silence and a pause. He thought he had imagined it, and was about to lie down when it came again.

Someone was evidently rapping softly on the door with his knuckles. It was an alien sound to Dromo. The door opened and he smelled food. He half-expected Antoine to be standing there and was actually startled to see a servant previously unknown to him carrying a bowl of something that gave off an aromatic steam. The servant, a young man with a bob of blonde hair cut in a straight line across his forehead, smiled and introduced himself.

"I am Alfredo. I will be bringing your food from now on."

Instead of striking the prisoner, or flinging the bowl in his face or insulting him, the young man deposited the bowl on Dromo's desk, gave a short bow and swiftly departed. Dromo hadn't dreamed it, the servant had bowed to him. Confused and disoriented, he made his way to the bowl and looked in. This was not his usual thin gruel. The food had the consistency of churned cream. It appeared to be made of some ground wheat or maize cooked in milk, sweetened with honey and studded with dried fruits. It gave off an exotic scent of spice.

The king had said there would be pudding, and there was pudding.

---oOo---

King Ludovico II knelt by his bed in prayer. His lips moved silently beneath the interlocked hands, knuckles rapping softly but insistently at his troubled brow. If God were listening, He would have heard not gentle praise but the most heart-rending appeal for help: not devout worship but instead the tortured cry of a desperate, lonely man. The only sound in the room was that of his mistress, Agnetta, breathing slowly and deeply as she slept on the far side of the four-poster bed that was almost a kingdom in itself. Who would be a ruler? In towns and villages and hamlets up and down the land, Ludovico's subjects slept as soundly as Agnetta, trusting in their king to keep them safe, trusting they would not be woken by black smoke and the dreadful roar of their hut being put to the torch. But he could offer them no such guarantee.

His anxious plea to God abandoned, he turned to the heavy,

leather-bound book on the bed, one of the two books seized from the monk's cell. He opened to the first page and read the book's title. Then he turned to the last entry. After studying it for a while he flicked back through several pages, glancing over the contents of the book, alighting here and there with a sceptical eye and a knitted brow. It had been some time since he had studied Latin and much of the writing that he found there was quite indecipherable to him. He could not share the contents of the book with his more learned advisors. He had decided to keep it away from prying eyes. He doubted it could help him in his present troubles but knew that a king, if he were to have any chance of ruling efficiently, must have access to secret knowledge. It was not enough to keep his enemies guessing, but also his closest friends, any one of whom could turn out to be a spy. As king, he had to take ultimate responsibility for every decision that he made. This was the way in which he would maintain his authority, both inside the court and at large in the kingdom. At the same time he must exercise caution, for the decision that confronted him now, if he were to be in error, had the potential to destroy all that his father had created.

What of the scribe in the tower, the rotund author of this work and the other book that Ludovico had destroyed? He, too, must be carefully handled. Above all the knowledge that the king had been alerted to his blasphemy must be kept from him. Ludovico had been careful to ensure that the burning of the other book and the execution of the odious scum who had brought the message to him had been in full view of the tower. The monk, who by all accounts had been cruelly treated throughout his captivity by this same vile wretch, would no doubt have rejoiced to see his chief tormentor hanged in his place, and this would soften his heart for the role that Ludovico intended him to play in the coming months.

Two books, one filled with heretical musings on the motion of the earth and its place in God's universe, the other an account of the trials and tribulations of his very own subjects. How such conclusions had been arrived at was impossible to fathom. What was sure was that the matter could not be overlooked. He would draw the little monk into conversation on affairs of state. He would have to work quickly to win his confidence. In this way, Ludovico wished to solve the dilemma that now faced him.

A decision was pending and it could wait no longer. He had at various times been on friendly terms with the leaders of the two most powerful neighbouring tribes, the Szarks and the Mendicans. His father had defended the kingdom of Metagoria from invasions from both when Ludovico was still a boy. Now old tensions had resurfaced, and it was taking all his powers of diplomacy to keep from all-out war with either or both of them. The whole region had become unstable, but recently he had met in secret with each of the tribe leaders, and each had offered to make a secret pact with him.

King Gustav of the Mendicans was a brutal, sadistic but ultimately honest ruler, whose word Ludovico felt sure he could trust, if only the two warlords could agree to the terms of their deal. Gustav promised that if Mendica and Metagoria formed an alliance he would, with not a trace of regret nor shred of mercy exterminate the Szarks, every last man, woman and child. He would lead his armies, with support from Ludovico, to the complete destruction of the Szark population, along with their culture, all known artefacts, or at least those that were found to have no intrinsic value, their language and mythology. In effect their entire history would be erased. Ludovico was in no doubt that Gustav could accomplish the task with his help, after which it was promised that peace would reign between their two nations for a thousand years. But what price peace, wondered Ludovico, if it was predicated on the deaths of so many innocents? Could Ludovico really have such a bloodthirsty killer for an ally?

On the other hand, if the deal was made, the world might be better rid of the Szarks, an altogether despicable race of liars and cheats. Ludovico had been approached by their leader, the self-styled Emperor Gascon, with a very different proposition to that of Gustav. Gascon felt sure he could broker a peace with the irascible Mendicans based on trade. The Szark lands were rich in minerals, chiefly iron ore, which the Mendicans needed to manufacture their weapons. Mendica, with its great, green pastures and lush valleys, was a mighty wool-producing nation, and Gascon was persuasive in his view that a treaty between the three kingdoms might benefit all, without a single drop of blood being spilled. Ludovico was inclined towards this Utopian vision and heartily longed for it to be realised, but for one small caveat: Gascon could not be trusted. In all his dealings with the unruly and egotistical Szark leader, Ludovico understood him to be true to his word only one half of the time. If he was lying, it could mean that Ludovico was walking into a trap.

The third option, to do nothing, accepting neither deal, was no option at all, since this could lead to one of two distinct scenarios, neither of which held much appeal. The Szarks and Mendicans could become allies, and turn on the kingdom of Metagoria, or else they might go to war against each other, with Metagoria as a prize for the victor. Such an outcome could end up twice as bloody as the one put forward by Gustav for destroying the Szarks.

Ludovico found himself helplessly prevaricating, momentarily leaning towards one view to the point of becoming wholly won over, then suddenly switching sides and favouring the other proposal with an equal conviction. He closed the book, placed it aside and climbed into bed. He lay back on the pillow, staring at the canopy above, immobile, paralysed with indecision. Agnetta, along with the castle's full retinue of lords and servants, ladies-in-waiting, dukes and earls, along with the people of the town of Boroglass and beyond, all across the land of Metagoria, slept on.

---oOo---

The first snows of winter had come, and they fell with a ghastly finality, like a sheet draped over a corpse. The land lay bleached, stark and featureless beneath its grey-white shroud. The great walls of the castle took on an opaque black, metallic hue. Dromo stared at the scene below, scarcely taking it in, so preoccupied was his mind with thoughts that tumbled and chased one another, supplanting all senses, rendering him blind, deaf and dumb. His food, brought to him by the servile and fawning lad who went by the name of Alfredo Duschene, was of a consistently high quality, of the kind served to courtiers and visiting dignitaries. It was something of a marvel that his former diet of bread and water could have so magnificently satisfied him when now the best that the kitchens could offer barely tasted of anything at all, was as featureless and bland to Dromo as the landscape he looked out upon. He ate it, nevertheless, for there was little else to do, and thanks to the richness of the proffered comestibles, he grew even fatter, even rounder.

Dromo now suffered a second of those afflictions that had previously been alien to him. Where he had first been afraid, now he was bored. He had quickly discovered on being returned to his cell that it was no longer locked, but this fact was of no interest. He had no curiosity as to what lay beyond the familiar routes down which he was accustomed to being led. And he certainly had no intention of leaving the castle, God forbid. Even if he had wanted to, there were always guards posted at every exit, but it never crossed his mind to approach them. Whatever Ludovico wanted from him he would endeavour to provide. If it kept him safe within these walls this was at least some small compensation. But meanwhile, Dromo began, slowly but surely, to feel what other prisoners must feel: the weight of the hours pressing upon him. He missed Antoine desperately, but most of all he missed his chief occupation, his reason for living, his studies.

Dromo was surprised to discover that the book he missed most was not his beloved *Doctrina* but the second one, *Fabula*. It must have been destroyed along with his book of graphs and equations, pendula and hexagons. Full of his moralistic musings on good and evil, *Fabula* had as yet no satisfactory ending, and no special point to make. There were no diagrams between its pages, no hypotheses or theories, every word being generated solely by his imagination. Featuring the adventures of the God-fearing but ill-fated townsfolk of Boroglass, this book had distracted him when he was unable for whatever reason to observe and measure the natural world. Some of his fictitious martyrs and miscreants had completed their quests, while others waited patiently for their goals to be realised or thwarted. Dromo tried hard to recall their strengths and weaknesses, their very human foibles, but without the book to guide him, it was a hopeless task. Like his mathematical equations, like the revelation of the hexagons, his stories were fast fading from memory.

Alfredo Duschene was as unlike Antoine Fleque as would be possible in any universe. Smartly attired in a tunic and knee-length pantaloons, with his neatly trimmed beard and regulation basin haircut, he presented himself at all times as the very model of a personal valet. In matters of etiquette he had no equal and he sought nothing from his life other than to serve Dromo with the utmost display of servile rectitude. He was respectful, courteous to a fault, punctual and attentive to Dromo's every need. The little monk despised him with a passion.

There was a knock at the door. There were only two reasons why Alfredo knocked, so very politely: at mealtimes, and to conduct Dromo into the presence of the king once again. This practice, which Dromo found very puzzling, was now becoming an almost daily occurrence. His personal servant waited patiently until his master bade him enter, then stood to attention while the monk composed himself. Since the terrible incident that had brought such misery and doubt to Dromo's life there had been several new privileges, if they could be described thus. As well as the food there were clean vestments to change into on a regular basis. There was hot water for washing his body, and from time to time Alfredo would play tunes for him on a lute. These impromptu concerts caused great annoyance to Dromo, though he had not the heart to refuse them. Despite all, the little monk was still possessed of a sweet, forgiving nature.

They walked together through the castle to the throne room. What Alfredo thought was happening in these meetings with the king,

Dromo could only guess at, and since it would be inconceivable for the servant to enquire, he would never find out. But it was immaterial since Dromo could scarcely have enlightened him. The king had a way of speaking in riddles. His questions were vague and rambling. Dromo ventured to answer them as best he could, but felt increasingly frustrated, not to mention confused, by the odd relationship that was growing between them. On this occasion Ludovico seemed in a particularly chill mood. The bitter winds of a steadily encroaching winter had penetrated deep within the castle walls and the throne room was cold, despite a fire that burned in the great hearth. Ludovico strode about angrily, barking orders to his minions who fetched more logs until the resulting blaze was threatening to escape the hearth and engulf them all. The flames from the fire added to the flickering of the candles in the great iron chandelier above, making the whole room dance with a thousand shadows. At last the king and his little unwitting advisor were alone.

"A philosophical conundrum, Dromo. It is indeed."

"Sire?"

"Two mutually insupportable notions thrown together, the unstoppable force meeting the immovable object. What happens, do you think, when they collide? Something has to give, am I correct?"

He brought his clenched hand down with some force upon the arm of the throne, hurting himself a little in the process. Dromo shrank back in horror. Ludovico glanced accusingly at him. It is a trait of very important persons that their foolish actions must always be attributed to someone other than themselves, as those who spend time with them are all too well aware. Dromo stared at the floor, as much to spare Ludovico's embarrassment as his own. The king rubbed at his bruised hand like a petulant child, and his voice became wistful.

"Here we see the throne triumphant. My fist cannot penetrate it. So with every battle there must be a victor and a vanquished, a winner and a loser. But what of philosophy, what of politics? When there are two courses of action, two paths in the road ahead, must one path always be right and the other always wrong?"

Dromo didn't venture to answer, assuming the questions were rhetorical, but a silence grew between them. Ludovico held his gaze until it became imperative that Dromo answer.

"An unstoppable force, Sire?"

"And an immovable object. What would be the result?"

Dromo thought for a moment. This question appealed to his scientific mind. He did not need to write down any equations.

"If they met, then surely the result would be the total destruction of both."

"Yes."

Ludovico nodded gravely. The answer did not satisfy the king, but merely confirmed him in his prejudice. And all at once he came to understand that he must share his burden. He had no choice but to elucidate, and here, in the person of the little monk, he found an unexpected ally. Whatever the monk knew – and his writings showed his knowledge to be extensive – he had exhibited not the slightest interest in politics. He was an enigma, a chubby aesthete, a genius even. But not a spy.

"I have to choose a path. One is very clear and certain, with a guaranteed outcome, peace for our nation. If I choose this path, many people will lose their lives. The other is uncertain. It could lead to peace with no shedding of blood, or it could lead to all-out war. Total destruction." He paused, then added, pointedly, "Besides myself, you are the only one who knows about it."

Dromo stood helplessly before the king, not knowing what to say or what to think. The supreme ruler of the land had decided to trust him with privileged information, demanding a response. Upon his answer, countless lives might depend.

"Well?"

But Dromo could only shrug. Ludovico lost his temper.

"You have no answer? Wretched monk! I should have left you rotting in your cell, on bread and water. Why so silent, when your writing speaks such volumes?"

And the king pointed in the direction of the fireplace. At first Dromo could not make sense of his action. His eyes followed the gesture but the room was empty, save for the trophies on the walls and the roaring fire. Was the king referring to the flames of the brazier that took away his beloved *Doctrina*? But he had punished Antoine for that crime. Dromo felt a pang of nausea, he swayed there on the hexagonal tiles, confused and flustered.

Then he saw it.

Dromo's breath caught in his throat on sight of the book, high up on the deep stone mantel that supported the bricks above the hearth. It was unmistakeably one of his own, lit by the orange glow of the flames below and the candles above, their light making it shimmer gently, eerily, as though bathed in hellfire. Dromo's mind raced. So the second book had not been destroyed! He wanted to rush to caress it, though it was clearly far out of reach. The mere sight of its bound leather spine was enough to bring stinging tears to his eyes. The fact of its existence far eclipsed the knowledge that the king was aware

Dromo had written it, the ramifications of which would have to wait.

Ludovico, however, would not wait. His voice was measured and cold.

"I will have your answer. Which path do I take? Mark me well, Dromo. As my kingdom is in the balance, so is your life."

No choice then, but to respond in the moment to the challenge set by the king. If he could touch the book, if he could only reach out, open it at any page, breathe its scent, he would know how to answer his sovereign, but he was alone, and helpless. He cleared his throat and spoke in a trembling voice.

"There is only one choice, that which spares the most lives. If certainty results in bloodshed, then uncertainty must be embraced, even at the risk of more deaths. That is your path, though it be a hazardous one."

And he fell to the floor in a faint.

---oOo---

A crack unit of one of the divisions of the company of the Emperor Gascon's personal guard was camped out on a hillside, taking a break from their daily drill, and watching the Emperor himself at play. Comprising just over a hundred men, this unit, whose skill was the crossbow, were lounging on the grass, laughing uproariously as their ruler humiliated one of their number by placing him in some stocks and having the entire outfit launch their leftover rations in his direction. It was an unusually warm day for this time of year, though the encroaching winter still made its presence felt by way of a stiff breeze that slanted across the valley.

The crossbowmen were a proud and fearsome band of Szark militia, who competed with other units for the favour of the Emperor. Such was the depth of their hostility towards others in the company it was said that they were more accepting of their traditional enemy, the Mendicans, than they were of their fellow soldiers. Indeed, had the man now presently in the stocks been a Mendican prisoner, he would arguably have been afforded more respect than the wretch whose face was now dripping with gravy from a well-aimed morsel of pigeon pie. Nor had the Emperor yet finished with this sport, for he was already picking another victim. The guard in question had no choice in the matter when his name was called but to climb swiftly to his feet and bow low to his ruler. The two men then spoke together, the Emperor clearly instructing his victim as to what was about to happen. Palini, positioned halfway up the slope of the hillside, could not hear what was being said so nudged his companion, a fellow soldier and bowman called Bassett, who explained the scene in between greasy mouthfuls of meat.

"The Emperor will make two statements, one of which is true, the other false. The fellow must decide which is which and then act on the information."

Palini looked baffled, so Bassett continued.

"He doesn't know if the truth comes first or second."

Palini nodded, thinking that he understood the test, if not the reason for it. Did the Emperor want to keep his men in a constant state of agitation, to breed fear into them? Or was this after all just sport? Below them, in the improvised theatre where Gascon interrogated the man, the stocks were being emptied of their previous incumbent. Then the assembled unit were treated to an extraordinary sight. The

Emperor Gascon, a towering figure with a shock of red hair and wildly staring eyes that seemed to look everywhere at once, stepped back with a grand gesture towards his chosen subject as if to indicate that the floor was his.

The bowman, who was clearly a little shaken, appeared to think for a moment, then, screwing up his courage, stuck his neck and arms in the air and began a strange dance, squawking and strutting like a chicken. A great roar went up from the company, and the Emperor Gascon joined in the hilarity, clapping and grimacing towards the audience of cheering soldiers. The hapless bowman, grinning sheepishly, came to the end of his dance, looking heartily pleased with his effort, until at last he turned to the Emperor. His face fell as their eyes met, for Gascon's smile had suddenly turned to a frown.

The Emperor gave a solemn nod towards the stocks. Two burly guards took hold of the bowman who went limp in their arms as he was summarily dragged over to the wooden contraption and clamped inside it. Then, after a nervous pause, the whole company gave a unanimous growl of aggression, like a pack of hungry wolves, and instantly began pelting the man with detritus. Fruit, pieces of bread, pastry and biscuits were thrown, the attackers taking far more pleasure in the man's suffering than they had previously in his dancing.

Sensing their mood, Gascon's demeanour had turned equally sour. When he searched the hillside for his next victim the soldiers swiftly hushed. Anxious glances flickered here and there. No man dared meet the Emperor's eyes, yet each feared to look away, sensing that this might also draw his attention. Had you asked Palini at that moment why his hand went up, he would not have been able to tell you, except that he was exercising his free will, an answer that would have proved unsatisfactory to the great majority. Perhaps it was curiosity that drove him. Suffice to say that there was an almost audible sigh of relief from the company when Gascon, with a sadistic leer, acknowledged Palini's outstretched hand, his companion Bassett shrinking away from him instinctively as though he had the pox.

"A volunteer," observed Gascon, and he crooked a finger at Palini, then slowly and repeatedly drew it back, inviting him to take the stage. Palini hauled himself upright and joined the Emperor with his head high and his jaw thrust out defiantly.

Palini had proved himself a worthy wielder of the crossbow, and seemed in every way suited to life in the Army. Though the bloom of youth had long since departed, he was still reasonably strong and his years of wandering had prepared him well for the long days of marching whilst carrying provisions on his back. He was a little stooped and his long legs clicked and snapped when he walked, though none of this slowed him down measurably. In any event those lusty Szarks who had recruited him in the tavern at San Gemini had clearly felt that what he lacked in physical prowess he more than made up for in bravery.

His toughest obstacle since he joined the Army had been the slaughter of his fellows, and in this he was at least glad not to have to exercise free will. In warfare these decisions were largely made for you. The enemy having been identified, your job was to eliminate him or face the same being done to you, either by your enemy or at the hands of your superiors. At first he killed with a heavy heart, knowing that the other man, as he charged towards him, had not the slightest thought for territory, or national boundaries, or political differences, his only concern being for his mortal soul. The battle cry was not born of hatred but of fear. This knowledge would not help you overcome him, however. In order to fight and kill, Palini soon realised, you had to trick yourself into thinking that the man did actually hate you, and everything about you, that he had no fear and would gladly give his life for the privilege of ending yours.

This was the arena of battle then, a field of brothers knowing only fear but showing each other only hatred. And then, when the fighting was over, it was best to leave the battlefield as quickly as one could, so as not to hear the whimpering and wailing of men as they died. Palini had seen dreadful scenes, with grown men calling for their mothers. On one occasion, two soldiers, one struck by an arrow, the other run through with a sword, cradled each other like babes in the womb. It scarcely mattered to Palini, and not at all to the two men, that one was a Szark, the other a Mendican.

Palini stood his ground, looking the Emperor in the eye. The watching unit was hushed. It was not the done thing for a man to volunteer for one of these games, and everyone watching expected that there would be some especially harsh punishment in store if this walking skeleton failed the challenge. Gascon leaned menacingly close to Palini, so that his lips almost brushed against his ear, and he whispered, with a small shake of his head.

"This is not my first statement. You are a brave man." Palini felt an initial rush of pride for having volunteered. The Emperor was confiding in him. He nodded respectfully and waited for the Emperor's first statement, which he imagined would also be whispered. But Gascon suddenly stepped away, turned in a circle, and after a few seconds fixed Palini with a cold stare, speaking aloud, so that those closest could hear him.

"You are a donkey, are you not?"

A ripple of skittish laughter ran around the courtiers and priests who comprised the inner circle of the Emperor's retinue. Several of the men whispered to others who clearly had not heard, and these passed the message on to still others until the whole of the hillside was alive with expectant murmurings. Then the Emperor spoke again, this time with an air of nonchalance, as though he had already tired of the game.

"My hair is a shade of red."

Palini felt his own cheeks flush red with sudden panic. Gascon fixed him with a devilish smile, a spider eyeing the fly that has just flown into his web. He held out his hands as he had done to the previous man, inviting an immediate response. What did it mean? Why had Gascon whispered so confidentially, so theatrically in his ear? What could his message mean? It made no sense. Should Palini now bray like a donkey, making the statement true? But it was clearly true that Gascon's hair was a shade of red. Not just a shade, either, but as red as a robin's breast. The other man had imitated a chicken, and he now hung limply from the stocks, doubly humiliated.

Seconds passed in an agony of silence, the only sound reaching Palini's ears being his own frantic heartbeat. Why had he been so foolish, so arrogant as to volunteer? His mind raced, thinking back over the challenge. Two statements, one true, one false, and you could not know which was which. What if Bassett had mistaken the rules? But that thought only further clouded Palini's already confused mind. Perhaps the hair on Gascon's head was not really red.

That was it! The hair was an unnatural colour. It must be dyed, or perhaps it was a wig. These were the only conditions under which his second statement could be proved false. Palini knew what he must do. He must throw back his head and bray like the most petulant, vociferous donkey that ever there was. No matter that he would make a fool of himself like the other man, for that man must surely have received different instructions, different statements. He would bray like a donkey, there would be much laughter, and Gascon would throw off his hairpiece and roar with delight. The red wig was all for show, a headdress for wearing into battle.

Then, just as he was about to leap into action, he paused. From whence the answer came to him Palini could not say, but come it did in a flash, and a great sense of calm flooded through his body. He took a deep breath, but instead of braying, he exhaled slowly, then smiled and bowed low to Gascon, whose expression meanwhile had switched from mild amusement to thunderous disapproval. The hillside held its breath at this astonishing display of audacity. But Palini would not bend, refusing to utter a sound, so Gascon spoke for him, quietly now, as though barely able to contain his rage.

"This is your answer, this silence, you impudent dog?"

"Yes, Emperor."

"I could have you hanged. Never mind the stocks."

"Yes, Emperor. But you will not."

"Oh? Why not?"

"Because I am a brave man."

Some awestruck gasps escaped the mouths of those nearest in the circle. Then slowly, mercifully, the Emperor began to smile, with the courtiers and the holy men and the scribes gradually following suit. Palini half-expected the Emperor's frown to reappear but instead he let out a roar of hearty approval. He grabbed Palini hard about both shoulders and held him tight to his bosom as the watching crowd erupted in joy and relief.

He had passed the test.

---oOo---

This doctrine of faith by which he exercised free will was working well for Palini, imparting to him the sense that he could do no wrong. Where before he had waited for God's instruction, which all too often never came, he now took bold decisions entirely of his own making, with little fear for the consequences. This seemed to bear out the idea, expounded by Edouard Apery, the Duc de Pomerance, that God rewarded self-sufficiency, that to act upon one's own initiative was in fact to do His will. Palini's destiny was being shaped by his own hand. He could feel God smiling upon him as he moved inexorably onwards. In a matter of a few weeks he had progressed from being a famished vagrant to his present exalted and envied position as one of the Emperor's most trusted guards. If that was not destiny, he told himself, then he knew not the meaning of the word. He had money in his purse, fine silk clothes on his back and everywhere he went he was respected, perhaps even feared by his fellow Szarks. A man could surely want for nothing more.

The Szark way of life, too, was beginning to grow on Palini. Szarks enjoyed a refreshingly spontaneous approach to life's pleasures, unlike their dour God-fearing rivals, the Mendicans. Szarks worked hard but played harder, their calendar consisting of what seemed like one year-long Bacchanalian festival, punctuated by unfortunate but necessary marching and drilling. In the evenings there was much drinking and feasting to be done, and the Szarks regarded it a duty to test their mettle just as much in this arena as on the field of battle. At one such nocturnal event Bassett, Palini's fellow bowman, of whom it must be said he was never entirely sober, lurched towards his friend, a bottle of wine in one hand and a rather alarmed-looking young wench in the other.

This took place just one day after the exchange on the hillside, and Bassett was still puzzling over it.

"You should have made an ass of yourself, Palini. You spoiled our fun."

Palini just smiled.

"Why did you risk your life?"

"I risked nothing."

Bassett frowned, visibly angered by Palini's show of arrogance. Palini was fond of Bassett, who had made a great effort in recent weeks to pass on his knowledge of the crossbow, so he decided to indulge him, though he doubted this was the right time or place.

"His first statement? The one about the donkey...?"

"What about it?"

"That was not his first statement. He whispered to me before that."

"Whispered? Whispered what?"

"That I was brave."

"Ah! And you took this to be true! But it could equally have been false, Palini."

"No, because that was in fact his second statement. He made a statement before that."

His friend was becoming impatient now. The lady on his arm suppressed a yawn.

"And what was that?"

"He said, and these were his exact words 'This is not my first statement.' That was meant to trick me, and it almost succeeded."

Bassett's eyes glazed over. Palini pressed on regardless.

"Assuming that this was indeed his first statement, then clearly it was a false statement, which meant that his second statement was the true statement. I was a brave man. So it fell to me to prove such."

His friend nodded sagely, not having understood a word.

"And the business about the donkey and the Emperor's red hair…?"

"Part of the trick."

Bassett then bowed low very grandly with a mocking flourish of his outstretched hand to demonstrate that he had been bettered. With that, he wheeled away unsteadily, leaning all too heavily on his female companion for support.

---oOo---

In times of greater sobriety the two men had enjoyed many private moments during which they had confided things of a highly personal nature. Palini spoke of his lost twin and the surviving boy who had abandoned the family home, and the telling of the tale brought back immense sadness, along with a measure of release for the pain having been shared. To Palini's surprise Bassett told the tale of his own brother, and greatest rival, whom he detested. This older boy, named Geraint, had taunted and bullied him since they were infants, and even now was never without an insult on his lips if he came across Bassett at crossbow practice. He would never miss an opportunity to belittle his younger brother, particularly in front of other men, and Palini found himself hating Geraint with almost as much passion as

Bassett to hear of the extent of his cruelty.

Bassett expressed the wish that Geraint had been born a Mendican. If that were the case he would have no qualms at all about killing him with his bare hands. When he made these announcements Bassett's eyes bulged out of his head and the veins in his temples visibly throbbed. Furious tears clouded his vision and he would many times have to stop mid-sentence to compose himself. Palini's heart went out to his friend, and many times he pondered how to help in the matter. But it is often the case that the bitterest disputes are those that spring up between members of the same family. There was nothing to be done.

Then by chance Palini witnessed the rivalry close up. One chill afternoon a group of perhaps a dozen crossbowmen, including Palini and Bassett, were practising their skills, aiming at a circular target made of straw propped up on a wooden support some distance away across a woodland clearing. As Bassett stepped up to the mark, enjoying a joke with the fellow shooting next to him, a tall, buckskin-clad man with wide shoulders walked into the firing range and sauntered towards the targets. A cry went up from the company who immediately recognised him as being from another unit. To encroach upon this hallowed ground was the worst breach of etiquette, even for a member of the crossbow unit, but for an outsider to do so was unthinkable. The man glared a challenge at the bowman whose job it was to retrieve their bolts, sending him shrinking away instinctively. The new arrival carried a pikestaff and sported a black beard that engulfed his face even to the point of covering his cheekbones. He looked like an angry bear as he turned to face the group across the clearing. Bassett was shaken to the core, and it was immediately apparent to Palini, and several others, that this was his brother.

In answer to a call from one intrepid soul for him to move, he insisted with a broad smirk that there was no need, and he gestured towards Bassett. He made the joke explicit by shouting that, with the present bowman at the mark, he could not be in a safer spot than directly in front of the target. The hatred that passed between the two brothers was as clear and as cold as the breath that came from their mouths in freezing clouds. Everyone present knew that Bassett was being taunted and there were many who could not contain their anger on his behalf. Some were muttering for him to shoot and be damned. Palini joined them. Not one man in the unit would think ill of Bassett for calling this bluff.

He pulled his crossbow up to firing position, which brought forth a gruff cackle of pleasure from his brother Geraint. There was a tense moment as Bassett took aim. Palini expected to see Geraint fall, for Bassett was an excellent shot, but there was the slightest tremble in his arm as the bolt was released, and it went sailing past its target at tremendous speed, missing Geraint and burying itself in the bark of an oak tree with a thud that echoed through the forest. Seemingly vindicated, the bearded giant threw one last insult Bassett's way and walked calmly off.

For hours afterwards, Bassett would not speak to another soul, less still with Palini, whose eyes he could not meet. Palini could well see that his friend was ashamed of his poor aim and the weak stance that had robbed him of the vengeance every man present had been silently praying for. He had shamed not only himself, of course, but also by extension every crossbowman in the unit, because Geraint would even now be regaling his own unit with the story of his malicious taunting of his brother. Palini was moved to anger and love in equal measure. He silently vowed that he would be avenged on this discourteous pikeman with the rug for a face.

Later that night, when most of his unit were yawning and heading for their beds, Palini struck out for the tavern where he knew the unit of pikemen regularly drank. He had no plan of action save that he wanted Geraint to suffer as his innocent younger brother had suffered earlier. He imagined walking into the tavern just as the tale was being told, his presence immediately silencing everyone in the room. Somehow he would find a way to humiliate this vulgar man in full sight of his companions, who would no doubt be so impressed with Palini's confidence, his panache in carrying out this worthy and principled shaming, that they would immediately side with the bowman in their midst and drink to his continued health.

Palini was riding high on the raw thrill of excitement that followed when he acted without restraint or fear of consequences. God, he knew, was on his side, and he could therefore do no wrong. As he approached the tavern, its glowing windows the only source of light for miles around, he could hear voices raised in laughter and his pulse quickened. Pausing for a moment to collect his thoughts, he came to the swift conclusion that a full-on assault of the pikeman within might not be his best strategy after all. He would go around the tavern and investigate from the rear. Stumbling through the dark over a knot of tree roots, he suddenly exclaimed aloud as he collided with a man urinating into a bush. The man cursed and turned midstream to see what fool this was assailing him. Even in this gloom the dark mass of beard was unmistakable.

"Geraint?"

Bassett's older brother was heavily drunk and confused. His pantaloons had slipped down to his knees and his urine was still splashing onto his boots. Before the hapless Szark could gather his wits, or his pantaloons, Palini took his dagger and without a thought in his head pierced him through the heart, killing him instantly.

---oOo---

It was a most unusual sight, so many flags and banners in the colours of both Szark and Mendica, a great multitude of knights on horseback in loose formation, row upon row of archers and foot soldiers standing to attention, the rival armies facing each other across a wide, snow-covered valley, the only movement the restless motion of the horses' heads as they bobbed and shook in the crisp December air. Between the two armies was a large, gaily coloured ceremonial marquee adorned with ribbons, and inside were the two rival leaders, the Emperor Gascon of Szark and King Gustav of the Mendicans. They were meeting to discuss a peace settlement.

Also inside were members of the Szark and Mendican elite guards, observing, if not actually overhearing, the intimate discussion between the two leaders from rough, wooden pews. Seated opposite each other across a round table the flamboyant Gascon of Szark was resplendent in his colourful robes and flowing red hair, while Gustav of the Mendicans was an altogether more self-contained figure, dark and foreboding in his bearskin coat, barely moving his head as he spoke, with hooded eyes that revealed nothing of his mind's workings.

Palini was seated some distance from the main action in the centre of the tent, not quite close enough to hear much of what was being said. It hardly mattered, since he took no real interest in politics, and besides, there was something weighing heavily on his mind. His eyes searched about the many rows of seated men for his friend Bassett. They had been separated early that morning in the rush to organise this unprecedented event, and Palini hadn't had a chance to confess his terrible sin of the previous night. He dreaded to think what he might say in his defence. He didn't know how the terrible finality of Geraint's death would be received. There had been no witnesses to the deed, and Palini had seen no extra value in confessing it to the occupants of the tavern, who would no doubt have slain him in turn.

Naturally he was given to hope that with such great animosity between the brothers, Bassett might be more relieved than angry, perhaps even grateful for the loyalty that this daring act of revenge had displayed. Then again, blood ties marched to their own peculiar drum. Sometimes love and hate become confused. Bassett had confessed to worshipping Geraint as a young boy, and it was this underlying passion that had hardened into hatred over time. The truth was that Palini himself did not know why he had killed Geraint. The murder had seemed to happen by itself. Perhaps seeing so much death on the field of battle had primed him to act this way. The killing had been mere reflex, nothing more. But what of his recent fascination with free will? Was it reckless, selfish abandon that had lent his arm the speed and force it took to despatch Geraint so mercilessly? Where was God in the proceedings?

Something was happening in the marquee. A furious-looking Szark official made his way through the throng to interrupt the two would-be peacemakers in their talk. At first Palini took no notice, thinking

113

this was all part of the negotiations. But as the man whispered into Gascon's ear Palini felt a growing unease in the pit of his stomach. Sure enough, the official made a gesture towards his ribs, using a cutting motion of his hand to describe what could only be a dagger's thrust.

Gascon's complexion grew suddenly darker, until it almost matched that of the stern Gustav. Looking as if he might lift the marquee up bodily and tear it in half there and then, he barked something inaudible at Gustav who shook his head, clearly ignorant of the news that he was just then receiving. Not surprisingly, at the rapid movement of both rulers, their respective guards leaped to their feet and for a few tense seconds it seemed that the scene would erupt into chaos, but Gascon and Gustav waved them down, silencing the general hubbub of agitated voices.

Gustav was speaking slowly, shaking his head with solemn conviction. Interpreting events with a wildly beating heart Palini knew beyond any doubt that they were discussing Geraint's death. After a little more hushed and guarded conversation Gascon broke off his talk with Gustav and scanned the faces of the Szark militia. The official who had originally brought him the news once again whispered in his ear and pointed into the crowd. Palini was relieved not to be picked out, then horrified as the mass of assembled bowmen parted and Bassett eventually came forward with a confused and fearful look on his face.

The events of the next few moments would resonate with Palini for the rest of his life. When at first Bassett was accused of killing his brother, his look of wild astonishment was pitiful to behold. The accusation clearly meant nothing to him, next to the unthinkable news that Geraint was dead. So now Palini had the answer to his question about how Bassett would take the news, and with that came the certainty that he had quite deliberately missed Geraint with the crossbow bolt, that he could no more kill his own brother than he could turn the weapon on himself. To think otherwise, to think that Bassett had felt shame for his poor aim of yesterday when actually the bolt had landed where he had meant it to land was the greatest folly of all, and Palini could hardly breathe for the truth thus revealed about his own reckless arrogance. He could not offer his military training, coupled with a righteous anger at Bassett's cruel treatment, as excuse for his actions. It would neither console his friend nor, it must be noted, would it save Palini from the gallows.

Perhaps it was simple fear that kept him firmly planted in his seat. With every fibre of his being he wanted to save Bassett. He wanted to cry out, to halt proceedings and confess that it was he who had committed the terrible crime. And there could be no doubt that it was terrible, judging by the anguished look on Bassett's face. By now the news had reached to the outside of the marquee. Men on either side of Palini were sharing it in disbelief. One of the most respected, most brave, most loyal of the Szark elite had been murdered. It was an outrage. Palini, despite himself, could not help but observe that only yesterday every single man in the crossbow unit had wished Geraint dead, yet here they were, all clamouring to praise him and mourn his passing.

Bassett was now pleading for his life, his face wet with tears. Gascon stood firm, impassionate before Bassett's defence, his ears deaf to alibis. He would make an example of this man, to show Gustav and the entire Mendican army that the Szark people could match them in their administration of justice. As Bassett continued to seal his own fate, Gascon and Gustav exchanged glances, and from the nature of these Palini knew without a shred of doubt that Bassett would be executed forthwith. There would be those, perhaps, who saw some justification for his actions, given the rude taunting he had received from his brother, but all would agree that the only penalty for taking the life of a Szark was death. He was led away, a shambling, weeping wreck of a man, while the words that would have saved him remained locked behind Palini's tongue.

---oOo---

This very minor incident, it was agreed by all, would not cast a shadow on the joyous event that the day had brought about, the laying aside of past grievances. A feast had been prepared and for the first time in living memory Szarks and Mendicans broke bread and raised their flagons together. There was much celebration, along with many good-natured contests and feats of strength. Szarks were found to be valiant and true, while Mendicans displayed a sensitivity and soulfulness that could never have been imagined before. These brutish men, who just a day earlier had been more than happy to slaughter each other on sight, now found themselves quite overwhelmed in their affections for one another.

Bassett could not take part, for he had been hanged.

Palini was alone, finding in himself no allegiance to either Szark or Mendican, wishing only that he could have taken Bassett's place in Heaven or Hell. He should have gone along to witness the execution. At the very least it would have served as punishment for his own sin to see his friend suffer the ultimate indignity, but he could not bring himself to go. Instead he sat welded to the same rough, wooden pew for hour upon hour as the merriment continued unabated around him.

Where, in all this, had been his free will? It had seemed to him that God had instructed him to speak up. If it was his free will that kept him silent then this surely marked him as a coward, in God's eyes and his own. Had he admitted his guilt he knew that what would have hurt him most, beyond the baying crowd demanding his blood, beyond even the noose itself, would be the accusing look on Bassett's face. He had wanted to avenge his friend, but had ended up betraying him, not once but twice.

As he sat there in his misery he became slowly aware of a presence at his side. He turned to see a shock of red hair above a leering, grinning face.

"Emperor…"

"Palini! Why so sad? This is a day for celebration."

"Yes, my Lord."

"I'm glad to have found you. We need to send you on a very special mission. If you succeed I will be greatly in your debt. You will be more than amply rewarded into the bargain."

Gascon had his arm around Palini's shoulder. Could he trust a word that was being said to him? Palini was wary, but what choice did he have?

"I am your servant, Emperor."

"This peace treaty isn't what it seems. We will need to …"

The Szark leader became uncharacteristically coy and reticent.

"… adjust a few of the boundaries that have been set. In order for this to happen there is one man who needs to be eliminated from talks."

"You want me to kill Gustav?"

Gascon roared with delight and slapped Palini on the back.

"My dear fellow, you amuse me heartily. You have such an impetuous way about you. No, not at all. He is truly my ally, and yours. He is a warrior and a soldier who demands our utmost respect. No, no. It is the King of Metagoria who is the fly in the ointment. Gustav and I have agreed to take that country, peaceably or by force, and share its bounty equally. But meanwhile our plans have been somewhat hindered."

"How so, my Lord?"

"We believe there is a spy in our camp, and this is making it hard for us to carry our discussions forward with confidence. We need to be rid of this undesirable element. I would therefore respectfully enjoin you to deal with the matter."

"With pleasure, my Lord."

"Good. I believe you're acquainted. His name is Pietro de Fey."

4
JANUARY

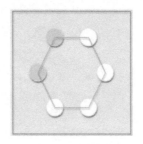

The king's armourer commanded as much respect and enjoyed as many privileges as those at court supposedly concerned with more spiritual, less earth-bound matters than the manufacture and dispensing of weaponry. It always seemed rather strange to Dromo, in his new role as special advisor to the king, just how very interested the clergymen were in the exploitation of gunpowder and grapeshot, not to mention the newest instruments of torture that were always being offered for the king's pleasure. The armourer, a bulky man who sweated constantly, no matter the weather, would be called upon to describe in loving detail just how some obscure leather and metal contraption would be fitted to the victim, how a screw would be turned, how and where a bolt would pierce his flesh, and so on. The pride that he took in his craft seemed to increase in direct proportion to the pain that each instrument would inflict, much to Dromo's distaste. But he was growing used to smiling and appearing to take his ease so as not to stand out from the crowd, just as before he had pretended to be morose. He reasoned that if his life in the castle had to be built upon deception, it was a small price to pay for his continued confinement, the thought of being cast out still filling him with an intense and suffocating dread.

"The powder goes here. My lord will take note of the metal lid on the flash pan, where on previous models there had been a leather flap. This innovation keeps the powder dry until the hand cannon is ready to fire."

All necks craned and all eyes focused on the item in question. King

Ludovico seemed well pleased and nodded with a stern, knowing, yet for the time being gracious air. All heads, including Dromo's, followed suit. The armourer carefully loaded the weapon and tamped the shot down with a long, metal rod. He went on to explain, more than a little defensively, that the gunpowder that had been newly imported from China was sadly less than adequate to the task. Thus having craved the king's indulgence in advance of the demonstration for whatever might occur, he proceeded to light the wax taper with which to ignite the powder through a small hole in the side of the barrel of the gun.

Dromo, for all his scientific curiosity, and despite his own stern, knowing, yet for the time being gracious air, was not especially interested in the hand cannon, knowing that its only function was to kill or injure a living human being. His role, as he understood it, was to read the changing moods as they played across his sovereign's features with carefully timed glances, and attempt to mimic them as best he could. So when Ludovico smiled, so did Dromo, and when Ludovico shook with anger, the little monk would huff and puff and stomp about without for a moment knowing what he was doing or why. And though he had been quick to gauge these changing moods of Ludovico's, and occasionally even to anticipate them, the truth was that his life had changed so dramatically, and in such a short time, that he hardly knew himself. No longer dressed in the humble habit of a monk, he now wore flowing purple robes, denoting his status as one of the king's most intimate circle. He maintained an air of lofty disdain towards the other courtiers, which mercifully spared him from having to engage with them on any meaningful level. He was quite confident that none would recognise him as a former prisoner, since he had always been kept well out of sight, and should any of the king's advisors even so much as look at him suspiciously, he would find a pretext to whisper something in the king's ear whilst fixing the offender with a look that sent them tripping over themselves in an effort not to give offence.

His meetings with the king had become routine to the point of tedium. They always took place in the throne room, and he and Ludovico were always alone, though Dromo felt himself to be under the watchful eye not just of the king but also of his surviving book, so far out of reach on the stone mantelpiece. Frustratingly, the king would sometimes take the book down and flick through its pages as if to remind himself of something he had seen there. What manner of consolation or solace Ludovico sought from what were after all just random musings on the lives of the little people of Boroglass Dromo couldn't say. He ached to be allowed to see the book, but he knew there was a specific etiquette to being in the king's presence. It seemed you were not allowed to move from whichever floor tile you had been placed upon. Thus Ludovico played with his courtiers and advisors as though they were living chess pieces.

In these quiet moments Dromo would respectfully answer the king's questions as best he could. The questions would range over matters as diverse as the weather, the shape of a bird's wing, or a point of logic such as his decision about who to trust of the Szarks and Mendicans, a point that seemed to have now been resolved, since word filtered through to Dromo that a peace treaty had been brokered between all three nations. But there were other, more sensitive matters that occasionally cropped up. One time the king had astonished his diminutive advisor with a question about pregnancy, specifically how one would know if one's mistress was infertile. Dromo's bewildered look was enough to end the discussion before it began.

Indeed this was a subject that Dromo would have gladly avoided, even had he known the first thing about it, since his relationship with Agnetta, the king's consort, was a troubled one. From the first it had been clear that her ladyship was no lover of little monks in purple robes, looking down on him with a contempt that made Antoine Fleque's former disdain seem like the most tender affection. Ludovico, to Dromo's immense relief, seemed altogether unaware of his lady's antipathy toward him. But then it was a king's privilege to disregard all whims and fancies save his own, and besides, he was not a man given to discuss such matters.

Many a time when Dromo was making his way back to the cell at the top of the tower, the key to which was now in his possession, he would chance to bump into the Lady Agnetta and, bowing low, would attempt a courtly smile, perhaps even a greeting, only to receive in return a withering look of pure disgust. Though it pained him to be out of favour with one so intimate with the king, at the same time he could not help but agree with her ladyship's assessment of him.

Dromo had come to see himself as a lost soul, helplessly dancing to the tune of an indifferent master, and utterly alone. He no longer grudgingly picked at the platters Alfredo brought him, but ate more or less continuously throughout the day, the ingestion of food being the only distraction from his misery now. He took no real pleasure in any of the dishes, though they were the best the kitchen had to offer, but nevertheless took a scrap of comfort from each bite. As a consequence the silken cord that fastened his robe had recently been replaced, its predecessor falling short of the task.

The cannon was fully primed and ready for action. A target had been set up a little way off at the far end of the battlements, and with the help of an assistant the armourer aimed the unwieldy device in its direction. He was sweating even more profusely than normal as he heaved the cannon into position and the crowd of curious onlookers instinctively drew back. These new weapons, cumbersome as they were, had many advantages over the blades and bows of the day, or so the armourer would insist. The longbow, in the right hands, was as accurate as it was lethal. Likewise the crossbow, which was more powerful over a short range but took longer to load and fire. A hand cannon was neither accurate nor easy to load but it more than made up for these deficiencies by being loud and menacing enough in performance to wake the dead. What did it matter where the shot landed, if the ignorant and superstitious enemy were driven to retreat from the man-made fire that spat from its grimy, soot-blackened muzzle?

There was a silence, made more deathly by the shared anticipation of its being suddenly ended. Then it came, a white flash of brilliant light accompanied by the most deafening thunderclap, which scattered the assembled courtiers like cockroaches before a lighted torch. Some flattened themselves against the floor. Others, more chivalrous in their nature, threw themselves protectively in the path of the womenfolk. Ludovico and Agnetta fell in a heap on top of Dromo as a plume of smoke rose high into the air. The fearful babble that ensued as people scrambled to regain some semblance of dignity was drowned out by a shrill and high-pitched wail of anguish. At first none could make out its source, the whole scene being shrouded in a pungent mist of burned gunpowder that singed the very air they were struggling to breathe. Then it became apparent that the screaming came from the armourer's assistant whose upraised hands were red raw with cuts and blisters. The man ran off in no particular direction, thrusting his bloodied appendages in the faces of the horrified onlookers, a wild and imploring look in his eyes. As the smoke began to clear and Dromo extracted himself from beneath the King and Lady Agnetta, one of the ladies-in-waiting screamed. The armourer had been upended in the blast, so that he appeared to be sitting quite contentedly by the outer wall of the battlements, but with his legs in a tangle above him, rather than below. In the middle of his chest was a hole where the shot had passed clean through, and his now sightless eyes seemed more at peace than troubled, more amused than angry.

---oOo---

The peace that reigned in the land, though ratified in word and deed, could not seem to penetrate the walls of the castle to warm the heart of its inhabitants. Szark and Mendican alike may have ended their hostilities, but biting winds and sleet and rain were not so forgiving. The winter raged on, shaking the southern tower to its foundations, probing every crack in every stone, feeling for the little monk with icy fingers. Where once Dromo had delighted in the shape and design of every single snowflake, he now regarded them with animosity, disdaining their ability to bond together in freezing, smothering blankets of frost and snow.

To make matters worse, Dromo's manservant and most unwelcome companion Alfredo Duschene continued to try his master's patience with an overabundance of thoughtful gestures, concerned interventions and heartfelt kindnesses. In short, he was a perfect nuisance. What most rankled with Dromo in his unfortunate misery and loneliness was the vast contentment with which Alfredo went about his duties, as if it were the most natural thing in the world to be enslaved to the needs of a wholly unappreciative and disagreeable master and to find in that pursuit the utmost fulfilment.

The truth, of course, was that Alfredo's happiness reminded him painfully of his own former blissful state, for it is in the nature of every man to want to see in the other fellow his perfect reflection, to want to share with him completely in any emotion, good or bad. This is what Dromo felt he needed now, a true companion who could take this overflowing cup of remorse from him and drain its bitter contents to the dregs. Not this grinning jackanapes whose pleasure in playing his wretched lute was as sickly and galling as the music that flowed from it. Whereas Dromo managed to contain his ire in large part, he could not help but show his displeasure on occasion, but this seemed only to encourage Alfredo, making him redouble his efforts to please the little monk.

As the days wore on, Dromo's mind returned again and again to the many trials and tribulations of the townsfolk of Boroglass as he had described and depicted them in *Fabula*. He felt a deep, almost spiritual connection to his fictional creations and even began to dream of visiting them in their homes, knowing that he would be made welcome there. How he would have loved to greet them, and more: to complete them, to see the just vindicated and the wicked condemned. His creations had been left in limbo, where he could not reach them. It was the least he could do since, by inventing them, he was the one who had caused that suffering to begin with.

Both books were denied him, but this one had survived, and

its continued existence served to give Dromo some small scrap of comfort. With the untimely demise of the king's chief armourer he had found himself volunteered as the man's replacement, so that his duties now included designing and building instruments of torture. This unfortunate turn of affairs demanded that he bring to mind one or other of the arithmetical formulae that had once counted among his most beloved companions. They had been confined to the flames, along with his trusted soulmate. But forget his accidental involvement in the death of Antoine Fleque, the true measure of how far poor Dromo had fallen from grace was his acceptance of the role he had been given to inflict ever greater degrees of suffering on his fellow men, and the truth of it cut him more viciously than the icy blasts of winter that ripped through his lofty cell.

---oOo---

Ludovico was at his studies once again, peering intently at the great leather-bound object that had so possessed him these dark winter evenings, driving out all other considerations. So absorbed was he by what he saw in these pages that he barely noticed when the door opened and Agnetta entered the throne room. She stood watching him for a moment before he sensed her presence, along with her quiet but persistent indignation. She stood with arms folded. As on many other occasions she wanted to know why he had not yet joined her in the bedroom, and was awaiting an explanation. Having none to offer, he simply sighed, closing the book gently.

"How could he know all this?"

She didn't answer.

"Where does a humble man of the cloth learn of such matters? Perhaps he lived before. You would need a past life to gain such insights."

Agnetta relaxed a little, thankful for the chance to air another of her grievances, for in fact she believed the two to be intimately joined.

"He is not so humble in my opinion, my Lord. And if it please you I would have him sent back to whatever life he once lived immediately."

The king frowned, half-mocking, half-serious.

"What has my little monk done to earn such harsh treatment, I wonder?"

"There is something untrustworthy about him. The way he smiles."

"What of the way he smiles?"

"Just that he is insincere."

The king shrugged. He had been smiling insincerely at his subjects all his life as they craned to catch his every utterance. What else existed in his world but insincerity? Had he not smiled at that mendacious Szark, the self-styled Emperor Gascon who had promised to make a pact with Gustav of Mendica? And had Gascon not smiled back and bowed respectfully as he left, with how many broken promises in his wake? Even now, when it seemed on the face of it that the peace treaty had been signed in blood, Ludovico could not rest. If anything, his anxiety had grown. Had he made the right choice between an honest murderer and a dishonest peacemaker? And who was it that had been his guide and confidant in this grave matter? The lowliest inhabitant of the castle, a self-confessed murderer, and a man whose presence in the throne room caused the king's consort to bridle and fume with anger.

"He is not to be trusted, my Lord. He does the Devil's work. He is always watching, and listening, though he pretends to be distracted. Pray tell me what is in this book of his? It has to be some form of witchcraft. Whatever it is, you have been beguiled by it."

The king knew full well that he had neglected his lover. It was true that he spent most of his waking hours trying to understand what he was reading, and when he did eventually retire each night his dreams were further haunted by the knowledge contained between those pages. He could ask the monk directly, but for the fact that it was Antoine Fleque who had gone to the gallows in his place. More insincerity. A kingdom was built upon such lies. He moved to place his arm around Agnetta, but she stepped away. He turned back to the book, making to close it, but then reconsidered. Perhaps, after all, her question deserved an answer. He hesitated for a moment before speaking softly, almost reverently.

"They are stories, nothing more. They shed light on the duplicity of the human soul."

"The soul of a blasphemer?"

"Perhaps."

Agnetta struggled to understand. She would not look at the book. The scratchings on the page would mean nothing to her, and besides, she vowed that should one of these stories be read aloud in her presence she would cover her ears lest Satan's words corrupt her. Ludovico noted her distress and spoke softly to soothe it.

"A man may be wise and also prey to evil. That is the message contained in the stories."

He took her hand in his and smiled warmly. She offered an enticement in return.

"Will you come to bed, my Lord? It is late."

Typical of his companion to shrink from his gesture of affection yet at the same time urge him to join her in bed. But it was her duty to lie with him, just as it was her duty to obey him at every turn. He was first and foremost her king, and she his subject. That he himself had not a single soul to bow down to was a burden he accepted he must carry with him each day. But accepting it did not make it less painful. Perhaps that's why he prayed so fervently to a God who never answered. Perhaps, after all, it was not the answer to the prayer that he needed, but simply the prayer itself.

"I will be there presently."

Agnetta curtseyed with as much decorum as she could muster and left, her footsteps echoing through the empty room.

The incident with the hand cannon had put his entire household on edge, the roar of its deadly misfire having resounded much further than the castle walls. It had taken an age for the panic to die down, and when peace finally returned the whole of Boroglass had been alerted to this embarrassing failure. There would be war, of that he was in no doubt. The only question that remained was who would be left standing when the last arrow had been loosed.

Those neighbouring tribes might have goods to trade, but trading was not the principal concern of a warfaring nation. They wanted to wage war, and there was no treaty to be made on earth that could prevent them indefinitely from staying their hand. Perhaps, after all, it had been better to accept the harsh terms of Gustav's deal, and let the Mendicans wreak havoc upon the Szarks. It would not stop Gustav from turning on the Metagorians in the long run, but it would have cut the potential enemy in half. Perhaps Ludovico's own militia, combined with the extra help of any mercenaries he was able to afford, could keep the Mendicans at bay for a while. He had no heir to pass his kingdom on to, nor did he desire one, for who in all Christendom would bring a child into this world, to suffer under the yoke of the very same burden as he had carried for so long?

There would be no Ludovico III.

---oOo---

In the royal bedchamber Agnetta drew the silk bedclothes around her and prepared to sleep. Her troubled king would not grant her wish this night, but would keep faith with another, more compelling mistress, one fashioned from wood pulp and leather. And though her silent prayer was for God in His infinite wisdom to keep her sovereign Lord safe, her heart sang an altogether different song, one that she would not wish to confess to her maker. It was a song of pure hatred, not for her king but for his new armourer.

She could trace her present frustrations to their source. Now her thoughts, softened by drowsiness, drifted back to that day when a manservant by the name of Fleque had been dragged up the wooden steps to the scaffold, all the while protesting his innocence. This filthy blasphemer, so it was rumoured, had been discovered making charts of the heavens in an attempt to disprove the Word of God. She remembered the baying crowd of courtiers, spurred on by Ludovico's damning words, demanding their bloodlust be quenched. Meanwhile she had looked on with a dispassionate air, wanting to join in but knowing that her role as one of the king's most intimate circle was to feign disinterest as the trapdoor fell away beneath the wretch and the flames consumed his evil book.

Later that day she had found the king ruminating over another great ledger, identical to the one that had been destroyed. When she had questioned him as to its contents he had immediately shut the book, casting an angry glance in her direction. She had humbly begged his pardon, after which his manner had softened. She had then gone on to remark that it was strange to think that the vile creature she had seen hanged could have been engaged in the study of heavenly bodies. In reply Ludovico had curled his lip, and something like a smile had played about his features.

"Indeed."

"A mere servant, my Lord."

Ludovico had looked intently at her then, evidently weighing up whether he could trust her with his private thoughts.

"Not a servant. A prisoner."

It was then that she learned the truth. Both books were the work of Dromo, the monk. Ludovico made no apology for the fact that he had sent another man to be sacrificed in place of the true culprit. Hanging a servant as lowly as Fleque was akin to ridding the castle of vermin, providing into the bargain a momentary diversion for the court as winter tightened its grip. Agnetta had known not to protest the point. Moreover, she did not fear for her own safety. Ludovico had trusted her with a terrible secret but it was beyond imagining that she would or could ever divulge it to another. Even if she did, her story would not be believed. She knew it, and the king knew it.

That only left the book, and if the first had been heretical, who knew what evil magic was contained within the second, despite Ludovico's reassurances?

Agnetta sat suddenly bolt upright in bed. For the sake of her beloved king, and for her sanity, she knew what she must do. The little monk had come between her and His Highness, King of Metagoria. Even now he could be plotting to usurp and enslave Ludovico. Either his accursed book would have to go the way of its twin, or Dromo would.

---oOo---

"Not hungry, Sire?"

Alfredo always spoke with the same lilting inflection, as though he were about to launch into song, which he very often was.

The food on offer was even more sumptuous than Dromo was normally accustomed to seeing. A large, wooden platter was piled with chicken pieces that gave off a sweet aroma. They had been rubbed with spices before being slow-roasted over the fire. There were quails' eggs in aspic, a terrine of venison studded with walnuts and olives, plus a generous bowl of some thick pottage that smelled like wild hedgerows. But there was no hurry. Dromo would eat his way through the whole feast, if it took him the rest of the day. For now he tore himself a piece of bread and chewed on it solemnly.

Alfredo plucked at the stringed tormentor that never seemed to leave his side. He smiled and nodded to Dromo as if in gratitude for a compliment that had never been offered and began to sing softly. How he managed to move his fingers at all in this cold, let alone play a musical instrument, was a mystery.

Dromo did not need to keep this lofty, windy turret for his home, but so far he had resisted every offer by his king to move closer to the castle's inner sanctum. At the height of summer, a season that now seemed so long in the past that it might have been antiquity, this had been a magical space, its curving walls a theatre of shadows, its conical roof a haven for insects, birds and even the occasional bat. Now it was dark as a witch's frown, cold as night-time on the moon. But it was the farthest point from the castle's great defensive drawbridge, and the much-feared lands and forests, mountains and rivers that lay beyond, so this was still home to Dromo. If it were cold in here, in Dromo's sanctuary, how much colder would it be out there in the world? His mind shrank from the thought.

While Alfredo sang he turned his attention to some metal pieces that had been in his possession since the poor armourer's demise some three or four days ago. He had been curious to see them at close range, and Ludovico had insisted he inspect them to try to ascertain the cause of the explosion that had caused the armourer to lose his life and his assistant to lose the skin from his hands. It was a purely academic exercise, since the king had already declared the longbow and crossbow as the two most effective weapons his army had at their disposal. He had naturally praised the armourer's endeavours, and admired his bravery in testing out this hand cannon, but rejected it outright as a useful tool of war. Nevertheless here it was, at least the pieces that had made it, in Dromo's possession, and he was, he had to admit, somewhat pleased to find that his interest in the observation of all things scientific had not entirely left him.

But was this part of the natural world, this instrument of death? God surely did not sanction either its use or its manufacture. Dromo turned the pieces over in his hand, this way and that, until he saw how they fitted together. Aside from the iron barrel there was the metal flash pan that held the powder, and a wooden platform that held the other parts in check. Perhaps it was the junction of these three component parts that had caused the infernal thing to break up at the point of firing. With a little effort, thought Dromo, and a slight adjustment to the casting of the gun barrel, the wooden piece could be done away with altogether, thus creating a more stable and effective cannon.

A sudden very loud twang from close by made Dromo's heart thump. For a split second he imagined that the gun had misfired all over again, but then he quickly realised that a string of Alfredo's lute had broken. Alfredo seemed equally shocked.

"Apologies, Sire. It must be the cold. I will fetch another string."

"That won't be necessary, thank you."

He had spoken the words a little too quickly, and now he felt almost sorry for his servant, whose one failing, at least in Dromo's eyes, was his unruffled, imperturbable nature.

"What I meant was, the food is also getting cold. I should hate to see it go to waste."

He gestured in the direction of the glistening plates, but Alfredo shrank back from them as though afraid to even look at the offerings. Dromo almost had the feeling he had insulted the young man.

"No, thank you, Sire. That would not seem proper."

"When did you eat last, Alfredo?"

"I have dined recently, Sire. I am entirely satisfied."

Dromo knew that he was lying. He had seen what Antoine and the other servants dined on: leftover scraps, vegetable peelings, chicken parts still with feathers attached. He wanted to see Alfredo eat. He was going to insist upon it.

He passed his goblet of wine across the wooden platters. There

was a silence, during which it became evident to Alfredo that he was
not going to discourage his master. Dromo kept his arm outstretched
until the proffered object was accepted. Alfredo took a small sip from
the goblet, and, after much encouragement from Dromo, a larger
one. Then, again after much prompting, he took a bite from a chicken
leg, chewed and swallowed. It wasn't too long before he had chased
that morsel down with some olives and bread, some quail eggs and a
great bowl of soup. Quickly his hunger overtook him, after which his
only difficulty was in finding the strength to stop. He helped himself
to plate after plate, pausing only to smile apologetically to his host.
Dromo, not wishing to see the fellow embarrassed, took a ladle of soup
himself and dipped his bread into it. They both chewed contentedly.
After a little while, and a little more wine, Alfredo started to relax. He
chuckled to himself, and Dromo enquired as to the reason.

"I should not say it."

"Say what, Alfredo?"

Alfredo took to giggling uncontrollably, perhaps unused to strong
drink. Dromo found it all quite amusing, so pressed him.

"You can speak freely. I will not betray your confidence. I give you
my word."

"The Lady... My Lady Agnetta... has been..."

"Say it."

"...has been asking my advice," he almost choked, "on matters
of love."

This did not seem possible to Dromo. The ladies of the court did
not fraternise with servants. And the Lady Agnetta barely fraternised
with the ladies of the court.

"I think you are mistaken, Alfredo."

"No. It is true. My Lady wishes to …" Now he whispered, though they were quite alone, and at least a hundred stone steps from another living soul "… She wishes to be with child."

This was hardly a revelation. But the chances of her wanting to share such information with a kitchen skivvy, no matter how prettily he sang …

"She told me herself. The king is not… shall we say, in tune with her wishes. She said that I would be doing her a great service if I would…"

This could not mean what Dromo thought it might mean. He wanted to close his ears, but then Alfredo reassured him.

"No no, not that. I mean, she wished me to enquire about a potion, a herb or some such that would … help."

"You mean an aphrodisiac?"

"To put in his food. She sought me out especially. Me, Alfredo Duschene. She said that if I helped her in this enterprise, I would be richly rewarded. But that I must tell no one. It would be our little secret."

"When did she ask you for this favour?"

"This afternoon, just before I came here. I was preparing these plates in the parlour when she appeared. She bade me go into the kitchen to look for certain herbs while she waited upon this very meal we are now enjoying, even stirring the soup in my absence. I think My Lady trusts me. I think she believes me to be true of heart."

"I'm sure she does."

And Dromo added to himself, though he didn't utter the words out loud, that she was clearly mistaken in that belief. But just as the thought occurred to him, he felt a sharp twinge in his lower body. He thought nothing of it, settling back onto his stool and rubbing lightly at his belly. Then came another sharp stabbing pain that made him gasp aloud. He rubbed a little harder but the pain only grew until his whole abdomen felt like a bubbling cauldron. Now he took to groaning helplessly, and he reached out instinctively to Alfredo for help.

Alfredo could not help anyone. To Dromo's horror his manservant had become a living statue. He sat rigidly, his eyes glassy and wild, his lips as blue as a kingfisher's wing tip. But it was his skin that most appalled the little monk. Its youthful bloom had disappeared, to be replaced by a ragged, waxy death mask, and his complexion was whiter than the infernal snow falling silently beyond the window.

---oOo---

The horse plodded on beneath him, its hooves marking time, barely making an impression on the frozen mud of the forest floor. Hunched against the weather above the nodding mane Palini marvelled at the creature's resilience, its stoic devotion to the task at hand. It felt neither the cold nor one vestige of the self-doubt and self-loathing that plagued its rider. How much easier it would be, he thought, had God in His infinite wisdom made him a horse instead of a man. He could easily see himself carrying a stick-like Szark warrior on his back. How much lighter a load would that be than this curse, this agony of human guilt and shame?

Two men, two brothers, had died, each by Palini's own hand as he saw it. The first death – not death but murder, he corrected himself, had been quickly over with at least. The second had unfolded by degrees as he watched, each successive moment as it passed condemning him forever. It should have been easier to watch a man hauled off to his death than to deliver the mortal blow oneself, but that was not true for Palini. And now he was preparing to kill for a third time, at nightfall.

His companion on the journey, the man whose blood he would soon be spilling on the frozen earth, was Pietro de Fey. They had been riding all day, from their home in Szark, across plains and hills, and now through the forest. Palini led the way, Pietro riding a little distance behind. Since they had first met in the inn at San Gemini, their paths had only occasionally crossed. The two men seemed to prefer it that way so had barely spoken on their journey. The frequent lashings of freezing rain did nothing to lighten their mood, nor could they have heard each other above the howling of the wind, even if there had been pleasantries to exchange. Furthermore, Palini feared any trace of intimacy with his victim. If he were to carry out his mission successfully, it were best that he consider Pietro less than a man.

"It's growing dark. We should make camp here."

Palini surveyed the area then slowly nodded in agreement. They had followed a stream at the base of a steep embankment where the overhanging trees would form a natural shelter. They dismounted, beating their arms and shoulders against the cold, and began to make their shelter for the night. There was no need to confer with each other. It had stopped raining, finally. Pietro busied himself with their bedding, while Palini foraged for dry wood to make a fire, no mean feat in this dank forest.

Palini dreaded the night. If the days were an endurance test, the nights were far worse. In his sleep he relived the moment when he had struck Geraint, willing his arm to stay, inwardly begging his sword to remain safely sheathed. Even in the realm of fantasy and dreams it would not obey, returning again and again to pierce flesh and cut through sinew, reminding him, as if he needed reminding, that what was done could not be undone. Then the torture of his shameful silence as Bassett was accused and condemned without trial, with no one to speak for him. There was no respite for Palini, nor could there ever be. As Bassett was led away in the dream, still protesting, the guilty man's nightly trial would begin anew, with Palini as both prosecutor and accused. In the daytime, when these thoughts assailed him, he could sometimes drive them out by concentrating on simple tasks, in imitation of his steed, the harder the task the better. At night there was nowhere to hide.

This deed with which he had been entrusted, the murder of Pietro de Fey, was no doubt another test of his loyalty to the Emperor. His travelling companion, it transpired, was not a Szark after all but a traitor, a Mendican sent by the king of that distant land to spy on the Szarks and report on their movements. How Gascon had come upon this knowledge was not clear, but the irony of the situation was not lost on Palini, knowing himself every bit as much a fraud as the other man. Indeed, since first meeting Pietro de Fey in that dark tavern he had lived in fear of being exposed by him. But fate had somehow decreed that he would live, and Pietro would die. Palini had long since ceased to wonder at the duplicity of Gascon, from whom he had known nothing but bluff and counter-bluff. To keep both friend and foe in a permanent state of doubt was clearly part of the Szark mentality. Palini had no political affiliation whatsoever, and though he knew he did not belong among the devious, lying Szarks, neither would he feel at ease with their vicious but trustworthy counterparts, the Mendicans.

He did not belong anywhere.

The plan was a simple one, cruel and callous in its conception. The two men had been sent on a bogus mission to reconnoitre this wooded area, the pretext being to find the best pathway through to the low coastal lands of Metagoria. Having set up camp and dined they would retire to their beds. Palini would then murder Pietro de Fey in his sleep. He would return to Szark the next day, telling of being set upon by a cut-throat band of brigands. Palini would then go on to explain, in some detail and with the appropriate degree of emotion, how he had only just managed to escape with his life. This was in order to prevent King Gustav from suspecting foul play. The traitor de Fey would have been despatched, and none the wiser.

Palini had built a fire on some flat stones by the side of the stream and rigged a scaffold of twigs above it from which hung several plucked pigeons, their breast meat suffused with herbs. When the meat juices flowed clear the two men ate together in silence, supplementing their simple feast with cheese and a little wine. Buried in their winter overcoats, they sat gazing into the ashes of the dying fire. Palini, who had little appetite, either for food or bloodletting, was the first to suggest that they turn in. If he were to carry out his grim detail, he reasoned, it would be best to get it over with as quickly as possible. There would be no ceremony, no grave for Pietro, no one to mourn for him. It would be a quick death, Palini would make sure of that. As with Geraint, so with Pietro: one thrust of the blade to the man's heart. With luck he would not even have time to cry out before he found himself in the presence of his maker.

Palini lay on his bed, ruminating darkly about his lot. At least, he reasoned, there were ample provisions. He had been generously rewarded for his murderous ways. His purse was full to overflowing, and the tunic beneath his overcoat was richly embroidered with fine silk thread. What a life of opposites he now led, a full belly but a cold, empty heart. The decision he had made to exercise free will had been intended to bring him closer to God, yet at every turn it seemed only to push him further away.

He lay in the dark, listening to the moaning of the wind in the trees above, punctuated by the shrill, far-off cry of some nocturnal creature. Then he turned his attention to his victim, a dark shape huddled beneath his blanket. Palini tried to listen for his breathing but it was impossible. He would have to wait, and pick his moment. A weary lethargy overtook him. His limbs felt heavy and his heart grieved for the deed he was very soon to carry out. Still, at this eleventh hour, he told himself, he might not kill Pietro. Did he have free will, or not? He closed his eyes.

---oOo---

Sometime later, exactly how long he could not say, Palini woke with a start. It had to be the dead of night; either that or he had gone blind. A muffled sound, a human cry, had reached his ears through the blanket of sleep. At first he could not say whether it was an actual cry or an imagined one, a product of his fevered imagination. But then reality flooded in as the full weight of a man's body landed on his chest.

Instantly, as two strong hands closed around his throat, Palini saw how cruelly he and Pietro had been used, and he cursed his foolishness for having ever trusted the Emperor of Szark. There could be no doubt. Gascon had charged each man with the task of killing the other, for nothing more than the entertainment it would provide him and his cohorts. Even now he would be back in Szark, drinking and laughing, patiently awaiting the arrival of the survivor, the final act of his plan to welcome him with open arms, and summon a great banquet in his honour. This was Palini's ultimate test, and he had failed.

In vain he tried to reach for his sword but his arms were pinned. He felt himself growing faint as the air was being slowly squeezed from his lungs. So be it. He had, after all, been prepared to despatch his travelling companion. True, he had had misgivings, but he would have obeyed the order had he not fallen asleep, and he would most certainly have shown a little more finesse in the execution of it than was being shown here.

Under cover of the velvet black of the night the treacherous Mendican took one hand away from his victim's throat and drew a dagger. A second later, Palini felt the edge of the knife blade against his throat. He said a silent farewell to his mortal soul. Then, suddenly, there was a flash of lightning. If only for a split second the whole forest was illuminated, and he caught sight of the man whose destiny it was to end poor Palini's suffering once and for all.

… It was not, however, Pietro de Fey.

In the confusion of the moment Palini somehow managed to utter his assailant's name.

"Ed… Edouard."

A mighty thunderclap shook the surrounding forest. At the sound of his name the Duc stared wildly at Palini, relaxing his grip on the blade. Both men panted with exertion. Even in his vulnerable state it occurred to Palini that he had not stammered, even once, since the first time he had met this man by the river, the rich man who went by the title Edouard Apery, Duc de Pomerance.

"Who are you?"

"My Lord. I am Palini. We ate trout together, and spoke of free will."

He had been prepared to die. In some ways it would have been a mercy. But yet when a man has cold steel at his throat, it is quite extraordinary how much value he suddenly will place upon the continued beating of his heart.

"We met by a river, not three moons ago. I had fallen asleep. You almost rode over me on your horse."

"Palini?"

As Palini's eyes grew accustomed to the dark, he could better see the marked transformation in the Duc. He was no longer dressed in fine clothes and his hair was a knotted tangle, plastered with sweat across his brow. The calm assurance he had shown previously was gone. This Duc was like a hunted animal.

"You stole from me."

It had only been two coins, and besides, it was in payment for the supper Palini had provided. He would not have taken them, had they not fallen from the Duc's purse, and furthermore, if God in His infinite wisdom had not placed them there, as a sign …

"Yes. I stole from you," said Palini. "Forgive me."

There was a silence, only broken by Palini's laboured breathing. The Duc's demeanour suddenly changed. He smiled to himself as he climbed to his feet.

"Free will," he murmured with a quizzical look, as if the words had some secret meaning known only to him.

He was evidently going to spare Palini's life, though he still brandished the knife. Palini glanced across at the lifeless body of Pietro de Fey. Pietro had evidently not had time to defend himself. It must have been his last mortal utterance that had woken Palini, alerting him to the danger. Now his hand went to his side, only to find that he had already been relieved of his money. The Duc saw the gesture and laughed aloud, revealing the stolen purse, which he had tied to his belt. He weighed it in his hand so that the coins clinked against each other within the folds of the canvas bag.

"You have come up in the world, I see."

And your fortunes have gone in the opposite direction, thought Palini, but said nothing. He moved to stand but the Duc drew a sword in warning. Palini's own sword was not in sight and had clearly also been commandeered. He settled back on his bed as Edouard rounded up their horses and climbed up on his own steed, preparing to make off. Just before he did so, he reached into the purse at his side and flung something to the ground at Palini's feet.

"Why have you spared me?" said Palini.

The Duc just smiled, turning to leave. But Palini had another, more urgent question.

"Are you really the Duc de Pomerance?"

"My dear Palini, if there is such a place I would happily declare it my dukedom."

And with that, he rode away into the night. Palini bent down to gather up the two coins that had been left him, the two coins that were all he had left in the world.

---oOo---

Friar Benedict broke the ice on the rainwater barrel with a sharp blow of his heavy wooden begging bowl. Scooping some of the crystal-clear water into the bowl, he took a few sips, then emptied out the rest and tucked the bowl inside his monk's habit. He pulled the cowl up over his head and trudged back through the orchard towards the monastery, his clogs making sucking noises in the mud. These winter months were the hardest for the order to which he belonged, and especially for the more senior monks. In summer his legs still managed to carry him into the town and even further afield to sell the various distillations that provided food for the brothers, but the cold made his old bones brittle, and he feared the treacherous ice underfoot, so in winter months he tended to stay close to home. This harvest had not been a good one, with heavy rainfall producing a stunted crop of apples that rotted before they could be picked. As a result the order was heavily reliant on subsidy from the townsfolk this year. The monastery would survive, as it always did, on charity. Whether he himself would live to see another winter was far less certain.

It was lucky for Palini that the friar stooped a little as he walked. A younger brother with a more upright stance may not have seen the outstretched foot, sticking out from behind a dilapidated, now empty beehive, attached to a stick-like, frozen figure curled beneath a blanket, too cold even to shiver. Palini's once fine clothes had all but perished. They hung from him in tatters. He could not have survived another night, or another hour for that matter. As it was the friar thought at first that he must be dead, but as he held the man's face in his hands, his eyelids flickered once, and by the smallest exhalation visible in the frosty air, the friar knew that Palini was alive.

He was wrapped in blankets and placed near to the fire in one of the innermost rooms of the monastery, below a carved wooden cross. Firewood was scarce, but here was a soul in need, and so the monks chopped wood to feed the flames day and night while they prayed for Palini's mortal soul. Too weak to eat solid food, he was given sips of warm goat's milk, while the two most elderly monks, Friar Benedict and Friar Benjamin, took it in turns to watch over him, sitting by his bedside with heads bowed. In this way he spent a full seven days slowly recovering from his ordeal. He had one other visitor throughout this time, a dog of some nameless breed, fed and housed by the monastery but belonging to no one. The mongrel was both scrawny and shaggy of coat, and went by the name of Sibunan, or Sibu for short. Sibu would often join the friars in their vigil, though whether he prayed for Palini's mortal soul was always in doubt. He did, however, give an occasional lick to the bony hand that protruded from beneath the sick man's blanket, and perhaps this in some way added to the efficacy of the monks' prayers.

In any event Palini lived, and gradually regained his strength. His aimless, hopeless and joyless trek on foot through a wilderness of frozen woodland came back to haunt him in feverish dreams when he would call out in strange unearthly tongues, so that the monks feared him possessed. In his dreams he would stagger from tree to tree, blinded by hunger, crazy with cold, until in some garish moonlit clearing he would stumble upon either of his two victims, the brothers Bassett and Geraint, sometimes both at once, their fresh blood weeping crimson ribbons onto the snow-topped ferns, their innocent, imploring eyes posing the same question, over and over: why? He had killed in battle, because he had been ordered to. He had killed men who hated him, or who had pretended to hate when in fact they knew only fear. But Geraint had not hated him. Geraint died without knowing the name of his attacker. As for Bassett, had he realised at the end just who it was that had betrayed him? Had he searched the faces of his accusers for the coward Palini, and deduced, in his final moments, exactly what had happened?

And asked himself: why?

When he was ready and able to sit up and take a little hot food, Palini made his confession, first to Friar Benedict, then to Friar Benjamin. The two old men were very different in manner and appearance. Friar Benedict, the man who had found him, was a stern, God-fearing preacher with unforgiving eyes who believed in hellfire and never spoke without a righteous intent to instruct the listener in the ways of the Lord. Like Palini, his face was chiselled, hardened by time and experience.

"You must throw yourself upon God's mercy, my son. When the Day of Judgement comes, as it will sooner than you think, you must be cleansed of all sin. For the Lord God is a righteous God, and He will know if you are unrepentant, and you will be cast down."

"Yes, Friar Benedict."

Palini took one of the two coins that Antoine had left him from his pocket and deposited it in the friar's begging bowl, from whence the friar took it and stowed it safely in his pocket.

Friar Benjamin, on the other hand, was a kindly old man with a monk's bald pate, a full white beard and small eyes that twinkled with unashamed goodness. He rarely preached, preferring instead to show by example how one might live according to God's laws. Palini never asked a question of Friar Benedict, but with Friar Benjamin it was a different matter.

"God loves you, Palini. God loves each one of us, regardless of our sins."

"But there is a Hell."

"Yes."

"I will go there when I die."

"You are already there, for God can make a Heaven or a Hell of this earth as He pleases."

"I am in Hell?"

"Yes. It would seem so."

"God is punishing me."

Friar Benjamin sighed. Sibunan yawned.

"God has no need, nor the will to punish His creations. The good will punish themselves."

"And the bad?"

Friar Benjamin paused to reflect before answering.

"There are no bad men. There is only Heaven and Hell."

Palini fetched the second coin from his pocket and dropped it into the friar's begging bowl, but the friar immediately fished it out and placed it back in his hand, with a shy nod of his head. There would be no charge for this counsel.

"Friar, how can I make this Hell into a Heaven?"

And now Friar Benjamin looked genuinely sad. He took Palini's emaciated wrist in his hand and patted it. Sibunan pricked up his ears in hope that he might receive the same.

"That, my dear Palini, will take a miracle."

---oOo---

King Gustav of Mendica was shown the body of the deceased. Pietro de Fey looked as old as time, like a petrified tree in a forgotten wilderness, his frozen corpse bespattered with dark, sodden leaves, his grey flesh pawed and pecked at by woodland creatures. One eye socket was a black cave, the eyeball freshly devoured.

The small attachment of Mendican High Command watched the proceedings from horseback. Others searched among the surrounding trees for further clues as to what had happened here. Gustav's lieutenant, a huge bear of a man who went by the soubriquet Justice, kicked at the ashes of the fire with a disdainful boot.

"There was no struggle, Sire. Our brother was killed in cold blood and left here for the wolves." He spat on the frozen ground.

Gustav's face was a pallid mask. In his hands he gently cradled the dead man's leather purse, now empty. The murderer had taken everything. He wrapped his robe around him, beckoning his second in command. The two men spoke in whispers.

Justice was the most efficient killing machine in Gustav's army. More than this, he was the living embodiment of the Mendican soul, single-minded to a fault, powerful in mind and body, with a determination to root out, torment and extinguish his foes. As ugly as a charred pig, he stood head and shoulders above every other man in the regiment, could hurl a pikestaff as if it were a mere dart, and was unbeaten in every contest of strength or endurance.

"Gascon has betrayed us earlier than expected. We must charge him with this foul act."

"No. He would deny it, and my nostrils are too full of the stench of his lies. We have made our plans. Our treaty must hold, at least until we have dealt with Ludovico and seized the Metagorian lands. Then we may have our revenge on Gascon."

The whole company had dismounted by now. The soldiers maintained a reverent and respectful silence as they formed a circle around the body of their stricken friend.

"Bury him with every honour."

Mendicans were as proud as they were brutal. Merciless in their taking of life, they saw no contradiction in the lavishly respectful burial rites that they reserved for their dead. Life was sacred, death more so. The lieutenant snapped his fingers and two men came forward to clean and prepare the body for burial. Justice stood mutely watching, barely able to contain his fury.

"At least let me take some men, hunt down the filthy Szark who did this."

"Impossible. His tracks will have been covered by fresh snow."

"Trust me. I will find this man."

Gustav did not need to think it over. He never doubted his confidant and right-hand man. Besides, revenge killings were written into Mendican law. He gave a solemn nod.

"Be warned this man is a Szark and will deceive you at the first opportunity. There is every reason to believe that if he does reach Metagoria he will alert Ludovico to our plans. Wherever you find him, be sure to leave him as we have found our friend."

"Yes, Sire."

Justice seemed almost to taste the wind with his tongue. He looked around the forest glade slowly. Swiftly making a decision, he mounted his steed, signalling to three others that they should follow. All four rode away.

It took a long time to break into the coal-black winter earth but eventually the grave was dug. The body, now wrapped in ceremonial robes, was gently lowered into it, and for several hours afterwards the forest rang with chanting as the soldiers paid homage to the departed spirit of Pietro de Fey, the Szark who was really a Mendican.

---oOo---

"He is a drain on our meagre resources. Had it been a good harvest, had this winter not been so severe...."

"Resources, Friar Benedict? Our calling is above such things. We are not a guild. We do not trade in wares. We have no resources."

The abbot and leader of their monastic order, Friar Jacob, spoke in a measured tone. He was a man both ancient and young, with a lined face and weathered cheeks beneath eyes that maintained their gentleness at all times, and a wiry, strong torso beneath his robes that spoke of a lifetime of devoted toil. Friar Benjamin nodded sagely, taking on the role of mediator between the two opposing views.

"Friar Benedict speaks wisely. These are difficult times, but we must remember that to give succour to a stranger is a blessing beyond material sustenance."

Friar Benedict scoffed at this.

"That much we have already done, but he is strong now. His appetite has returned and we cannot meet its demands. I say let him go."

"We will wait another day or two before deciding his fate."

The abbot had spoken, and the meeting adjourned.

Palini's appetite had indeed returned, but still he ate little better than the dog, Sibunan, who had become, in the space of a few days, his most loyal and trusted friend. They had established something of a routine. Man and dog would leave the monastery at first light, Palini looking like a scarecrow in the rough habit he had borrowed which barely covered his knees. Sibunan did not appear to judge him or even make the slightest reference to his new master's gangly appearance. Together they would forage for berries or nuts, or perhaps attempt to rudely interrupt a squirrel's hibernation, while his benefactors first prayed for food then begged for it in the marketplace of the nearby town. Palini, being unsuited to either of these humble disciplines, proposed to Friars Benedict and Benjamin that he would sooner hunt for the food, if this found favour with the two of them. Friar Benjamin was not offended but merely laughed, pointing out that if Palini came back with something to eat then their prayers had indeed been worthwhile. Friar Benedict was not amused, saying that he did not pray for food, but for salvation.

Palini came to understand the way the two senior monks got along, often parrying or even flatly contradicting each other's statements. Despite being apparently at odds in every respect, they tolerated each other's views well enough and, Palini suspected, may have even enjoyed the game. He once asked Friar Benjamin why Friar Benedict was always angry.

"Friar Benedict believes that God is angry at his creation for its fall from grace. Therefore Friar Benedict is angry on God's behalf. In expressing anger Friar Benedict is doing God's work."

"But you are not angry, Friar Benjamin."

"I do God's work in my own way."

"Because God is love, and so you love everyone?"

Friar Benjamin laughed again, nodding.

"Even Friar Benedict."

"But one of you must be wrong."

"Not at all. It is quite normal to feel love and anger at the same time. Besides which, anything is possible for God. Have you never felt these two contradictory emotions at precisely the same time?"

Palini thought of his son Matthew, now lost to him. But the memory was too painful, and so slipped his mind as nimbly as the squirrel he had seen escaping from one of the traps he had laid earlier that day. Friar Benjamin twinkled on.

"God is all things, all emotions, all feeling. We poor humans can mostly deal with but one emotion at a time."

"I hate Friar Benedict."

The words left his mouth before he could censor them, but they seemed to cause Friar Benjamin not the slightest upset. He replied quickly, but without malice.

"And that is how Palini does God's work." He added with the most forgiving of smiles, "…But that may change."

---oOo---

Palini was returning from his day's hunt with Sibu at his side, making his way slowly through the sprawling orchard in the field above the monastery, which now loomed up ahead, half-submerged among thick trees. He was lost in thought, remembering the dead man he had left behind in the woods. Pietro had been a spy, but he felt only pity for him, mixed with a certain relief that he had not after all had to deal the fatal blow himself. Still, it had been a strange, brutal twist of fate, and the fact that he had had no means of breaking the soil of the forest floor sufficiently to bury Pietro weighed heavily.

Suddenly a distressed Friar Benjamin waved to him, pressing a finger to his lips. Palini knew that there was trouble. Friar Benjamin never normally seemed anything but serene. It was early afternoon, not quite ten days since Palini's arrival in their midst, and the monks had been going about their business, preparing to go into the town with their begging bowls, when the call had gone out that they had visitors.

The lieutenant and his entourage were clearly bent on revenge. Each man was heavily armed and each surveyed the monastery's ancient crumbling walls with murderous intent. Justice had called the abbot out and Friar Jacob had answered. The two men were now in discussion in a clearing at the entrance to the main building, the abbot's dignified, upright frame dwarfed by the Mendican's towering bulk. Palini had been quickly ushered inside. Now he and Friar Benjamin joined Friar Benedict at a window and peered out, making sure to stay hidden from view.

Only the faintest sounds met their ears but Palini didn't need to hear what was being said to know that these men were pursuing him, that they'd tracked him here. From his vantage point he could just make out their leader, a man with a face so scarred and pitted that it might be a map of the moon. Friar Jacob's calm demeanour was in sharp contrast to the snarling of Justice, who seemed almost to spit in the holy man's face as he made his demands. There was much gesticulating in the direction of the monastery building, and Palini grew increasingly distressed.

"The abbot is giving me away."

Friar Benjamin's face was grave.

"The brother will not lie. But you have sanctuary with us. They are forbidden to enter."

Friar Benedict said nothing, but his lips betrayed the trace of a sardonic smile. Palini could stand the tension no longer. He had proved himself a coward once. To do so again was intolerable.

"I must go out there."

Both friars moved to detain Palini, but as they did so, a movement outside stopped all three men in their tracks. Friar Jacob was now walking away from the lieutenant, and slowly, very patiently making his way back inside. In a few moments he appeared before them. In his neutral tones he explained what had gone on. The Mendicans had indeed traced Palini to the monastery, and wanted his blood. But Friar Jacob had persuaded him to let one of the friars speak in defence of their guest. If he succeeded, the Mendicans would leave without exacting their revenge.

"Palini, you must choose an advocate, one of these two friars who will speak for you."

Palini shook his head violently.

"I cannot let anyone risk such a thing for me. The Mendicans are savage."

Even Sibunan was alert to the tension in the room. He gave a low growl of disapproval. Palini looked helplessly at Friar Jacob, but the abbot remained implacable. He now turned to Friar Benjamin.

"Well, then… if I must choose…"

Friar Benjamin accepted the challenge with perfect grace, pausing only to lay a reassuring hand on Palini's arm.

"All will be well."

Moments later, Friar Benjamin, looking pitifully frail and old next to the brutish Mendican lieutenant, was standing bathed in a patch of pale sunlight as he spoke for the wanderer, his bald patch gleaming in the centre of the halo-like ring of white hair. Once again the onlookers could not make out his words. His back was turned to them, but as he made his customary small gestures with his wrinkled but expressive hands, Palini knew full well that he would be smiling broadly as he delivered his testimony. As for Justice's reaction to the sermon, it was harder to predict. He seemed less moved than bemused, and frequently enjoined his fellow officers to appreciate the sentiments on offer. Soon they were clapping each other on the back and wiping away tears of laughter. Friar Benjamin seemed to revel in their obvious enjoyment, and his gestures became ever more expansive until, with no warning at all, Justice produced a club and brought it down with full force upon the friar's head.

Friar Benjamin slumped to the ground with the force of a sack of grain and did not move. There was a collective gasp of horror from the onlookers at the window, whose numbers had been swollen by several others of the order, and panic spread through them like wildfire. Palini let out a cry of pain that instantly reached the ears of Justice. He looked directly at their window and as he did so his men swarmed as one towards the monastery.

Father Benedict had gripped Palini's arm and was half-leading, half-carrying him towards an exit. Palini protested.

"Let me go."

"That's what I am doing. It's what I wanted all along."

The ancient oak door leading to the orchard was stiff, but Friar Benedict wrestled it open with surprising force and almost hurled

Palini out into the cold.

"I don't understand," Palini said. "If I don't go with them, you might all be killed."

"That is in God's hands."

"But… it's me they want. I must do this… for Friar Benjamin."

Now Friar Benedict fixed him with a steady gaze.

"What I do now, I do for Friar Benjamin."

Palini could not speak for gratitude. His stammer returned.

"This is the m… miracle Father Benjamin spoke of."

"There are no miracles," said Friar Benedict flatly.

"You're a holy man. How … ca… can you say that?"

The old man was heaving the door shut. Only his sharp features remained in view, peering over his knuckles as they gripped its outer edge.

"Because everything is a miracle. Now run."

The door slammed shut.

5
FEBRUARY

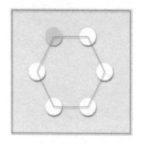

It had been winter for so long that it seemed the whole world had forgotten how to breathe, how to laugh or turn its face to Heaven. The sun, in those rare moments when it appeared, did not illuminate the sky but threw a sickly pallor over grass and stone, wood and water, land and sea. Colours had retreated before its malignant dead stare; shadows, too, had fled.

There were now two deaths on Dromo's conscience, two innocents whose association with the monk in the high tower had brought about their ends. He blamed himself, though he had intended neither for Antoine Fleque to go to the gallows, nor for Alfredo Duschene to be so horribly poisoned that he had turned into a corpse before he even had time to feel pain. Dromo himself had lain sick of a fever for several days after ingesting just a mouthful of the tainted soup, but this hardly compensated for the fact that it was he who had forced the food upon his servant. And when he thought back to the many times he had wished Alfredo to be gone for good, for his infernal singing to cease forever, his guilt was compounded. That the Lady Agnetta had laced the platter with a vile compound was in no doubt, but he could only see the part that he had played in Alfredo's demise. Her Ladyship's attempt on his own life was a mystery too deep to fathom. Perhaps she saw through his purple robes of office to the black heart that lay beneath. If only she'd succeeded in her task.

He would not move his bed from the increasingly chilly tower, and he refused all offers of another servant to replace Alfredo. For the first time in his admittedly formless memory he knew himself to be outcast and unloved, for once truly a prisoner, though his cell door remained unlocked. At night he pressed himself against the cold, hard floor and blinked into the darkness, finding the effort of trying to sleep more tiring than staying awake. On those occasions he would gaze up at the full moon with none of his former sense of wonder, but merely wishing its baleful glare could swallow him whole.

Only one thing had changed: his appetite. For the first time ever he indulged himself, partaking indiscriminately of whatever was on offer. At almost any hour of the day he could be found, always alone, sitting hunched over a bowl of broth in a corner of the great kitchen. He seemed to take no pleasure from the activity, and was largely ignored by the cooks and servants who toiled there. Those who did whisper about him, always out of earshot, speculated that he was attempting more to drown than to feed himself. He knew they feared him, so would not approach, except when ordered to bring more food.

When he wasn't at his trough he busied himself in the service of his king, for whom he had become, by degrees, chief advisor in matters of the defence of the realm. Alfredo's death and his own temporary fever had been attributed to natural causes and was never questioned, while Dromo kept a discreet distance from the king's consort, avoiding her whenever possible, and when in her presence assuring that he never made eye contact. Each night, when he was finally dismissed, he would bow to his sovereign and with a humble expression of gratitude for the day's work creep slowly back to his icy tower, his former sanctuary up the spiral stairway that seemed to go on forever.

---o0o---

"And what is this for?"

"It is called a ratchet, Sire. As the wheel turns and the ropes take up the slack, this metal pin engages with another tooth on the rim, and you can see that once engaged the ratchet cannot turn back so it holds the rope taut."

Dromo motioned to a servant to demonstrate. On the middle of the wooden slab a pig's dismembered leg had been attached at both ends to two circular drums, one at each end of the table. As the servant turned the large wheel so the ropes pulled on the leg, putting a strain on the joint holding upper and lower bones together. The ratchet wheel also turned until the metal pin halted its motion with an audible clank.

"Again."

One more turn of the wheel and the joint of meat shuddered visibly. There was a sharp pop as the knee bone detached itself, then as the wheel turned a third time there was a subtle but still audible rending of tissue until the joint suddenly gave way, separating into two bloodied stumps with flaps of skin loosely attached. Ludovico was swept with a sudden nausea, fancying he could hear the screams of the man whose body would stand in for this pig's leg on the rack.

He did not want war, but had been alive long enough to know that what he wanted counted for little. War, he had long concluded, was man's natural state; peace only ever a temporary cessation of hostilities. Signing the treaty with the Szarks and Mendicans had only increased his anxiety, as he had suspected it would. Trade was thought by many an idle occupation in these troubled times, prosperity itself a chimera. Why build relationships for the sake of trade when you could simply wage war on another nation and help yourself to all of its resources? War was deeply ingrained in human nature. War was the sport that men craved, and leaders of men especially, so any offer of peace must be viewed as a ploy designed to make Ludovico lower his defences.

How he envied the little monk his wisdom, heretical or not! He often wondered how a lowly prisoner had come by such esoteric knowledge as set down in the book that he had now purloined for himself, the book that rarely left his side. This gift for learning was truly something to be marvelled at. He himself was a simple man, though not entirely witless, his main strength being that he knew himself to be weak, possessing few, if any, regal qualities whatever. This was, he supposed, inevitable in a system that favoured the bloodline above all else. He did not doubt his Divine Right to the throne, which had been a tenet of his existence since he had first drawn breath, but from an early age he had wondered if some terrible mistake had been made, for he did not feel himself to be a king in word or deed. In a test of physical strength or daring, he would surely have fallen at the first, and thereafter been grateful to be seated with the rabble, cheering on the winners. He did not have his father's taste for battle and so was forced to find solutions in diplomacy. But here, with opponents like Gascon of Szark, whose every utterance was charged with double meanings and duplicity, here even the little monk's book of knowledge could shed no light, could offer no advice. And above all else, Ludovico II hated making a decision on his own.

He turned back to his diminutive armourer and defence minister, his unblinking stare masking the disgust he felt for the instrument of torture.

"This design… It meets with your approval?"

"Oh yes, Sire," said Dromo dutifully. "It is a fine example of the type, with many outstanding features. I do approve of it with all my heart."

Six Moons

---oOo---

Dromo was alerted to her approach from her very first footfall on the very first step. His ears had been attuned over an eternity to the echoing of footsteps on stone. How often had he waited while his faithful, now sorely betrayed old friend Antoine Fleque had ascended with his broken, limping gait, the sound of his exhausted clambering punctuated by curses that would shame the Devil. So different from the measured steps of poor Alfredo Duschene, who crept upwards silently so as not to disturb his master, yet always managed to do so. This sound was different again. The footfalls were slow and hesitant, light and delicate, but no less menacing for that. It could not be anyone but the Lady Agnetta, come to finish the task that she had begun, to dispose of the little monk. Not for the first time did Dromo silently wish for the end to be swift and painless. This time she would not come with poison but with a blade, he guessed, and gracefully feminine though she was, she would meet with no resistance from her intended victim, but only gratitude. His one hope was for a few precious seconds before the sword's deliverance in which he might beg for and receive forgiveness from this lovely princess, this queen-in-waiting, whom he had so aggrieved.

It took an age for the door to his cell to swing slowly open. Agnetta stood there staring down at him, her blank expression of horror or hatred – he could not be sure which – boring into his soul. She carried no blade. She would despatch him with her bare hands, such was her loathing for the monk. Dromo tried to summon words but her ladyship spoke first.

"Please… You must … forgive me."

And she fell to her knees, tears welling in her eyes and spilling instantaneously down her cheeks. As fast as the tears flowed, so did her confession, a long and heartfelt account of her sinful plot against Dromo, inspired by the many hours and days her lover had been a slave to his book. It had taken the death of an innocent manservant for her to realise her error, this young minstrel whom she had grown so fond of in the execution of her plan, winning his trust with a bogus claim to be interested in love potions. While thus distracting him, she had laced Dromo's supper with poison.

It was fitting, she concluded, that her punishment for the attempt to kill a man for whom she felt nothing but contempt was to kill another for whom she was almost maternally fond. God, in His infinite wisdom, had opened her eyes to the common humanity of all. Now, her confession heard and the well of sorrow spent, she sat with the monk for a while in quiet contemplation. She regretted her deeds with such painful sincerity that Dromo fought the urge to embrace her. Finally she spoke.

"I watched over you." She wiped a tear-stained hand across her cheek.

"My Lady…?"

"When you were sick. I tended you for a while, until the fever subsided. You looked so helpless lying there, so vulnerable. I knew that, if you lived, I would do all in my power to make amends."

Dromo was lost for words. But to withhold his favour was not in his gift.

"I forgive you."

She smiled sweetly, then flashed him an almost sly, conspiratorial look.

"There was a word, a name, you murmured to yourself, hour after hour. Do you know what that was?"

It could only be one thing, and it was not a name but the geometric shape that had so intrigued him in the throne room. Had he been babbling like a lunatic in her presence?

"Hexagon, my Lady?"

Agnetta shook her head, bewildered and just a little annoyed.

"It was a maiden's name. Margery."

---o0o---

He saw her at the bakery that she ran with her father by the millstream. His confusion from the start could not be more acute, for though he had lain abed with several fair maidens, yet he had never known true love, and so the introspection and self-doubt that accompanies such strong emotion took him by surprise. His first thoughts were more angry than loving, his head being suddenly filled with questions of a wholly ungracious nature that quite defied logical analysis. What right had she to be so lovely after all? From whence had she sprung? And why had he not been informed of her presence here until now? How dare she force upon him this dreadful awkwardness, this terrible bashfulness? Never had his body felt so rebellious, his limbs so ungainly, his tongue so inadequate of speech. Above all, what must he do next, for surely these feelings, whatever they were, would have to be dealt with, could never be ignored? His heart sank with the weight of it all.

And yet his heart soared. Passing him a loaf of bread, she took his coin and he felt the heat of her hand. Their eyes met and he foolishly averted his gaze for fear of crying out loud. He wanted to weep in her arms and tell her everything. Instead he frowned with unbridled fury and could not have spoken if his very life had been at stake. When she was gone from his sight he longed for a glimpse of her again, though had he been asked he could not have described one detail of her appearance. Hair dark? Eyes brown? Or were they blue? No one aspect of her being could be singled out for special praise. But the sum of those parts transformed her, and him.

He lay awake, thinking of her, his nightshirt damp with sweat. He grew morbid in his outlook, knowing that he would have her at all costs, yet fearing that he would lose her, too. What kind of witchcraft could make a man nostalgic for a love that he had not yet tasted, mourning its loss before he had even spoken one word to the maiden in question?

One word. What to say? What would they be, his first words to Margery? This was a question he had never asked himself before of any maid. His passion had been too quickly recognised in the past, too hungrily indulged, too easily quenched. This love was of another order, and it frightened him and enchanted him in equal measure. Was it possible? Could there exist a passion so incandescent that it could not be dimmed? And would that be a good or an evil thing?

He had the speech prepared. It would be bold but not forthright, flattering but not ingratiating, fond but not fawning. When she asked him his business he forgot every word of it.

"Are your muffins fresh?"

She giggled, and he felt himself turn crimson with shame. This was not wooing, nor even being wooed. He wanted to die, but not yet, dear God, not yet.

---o0o---

Dromo welcomed the invasion of his privacy, even though by her own admission the Lady Agnetta had tried to kill him. What did it matter when his own life was forfeit? He had lost his precious *Doctrina* and with it his fascination with the world both inside and outside his lofty laboratory. He had gone from the lowly position of a prisoner to an even lowlier one as the servant of a king whose only motivation, so it seemed, was to wage war and inflict pain. Dromo, the little monk whose joy at being alive had been matched only by his love for all other humans, good and bad, was reduced to this: he had become a torturer because he could not face the alternative, to leave the castle, his home.

After that first encounter with his queen there followed many others, and on each occasion there would be vouchsafed to Dromo some new confidence, some fresh and intimate detail of her life as a royal consort, broadening and extending his understanding of the workings of the king's household and deepening the trust that was slowly building between them. Agnetta seemed to have been freed of some invisible burden after her failed assassination attempt, as though in order to really trust him, she needed first to have sinned against him. They shared a secret bond, this novice murderer and her intended victim, and quite soon it became clear that they shared something else besides, for Agnetta's loneliness was equal to Dromo's in every particular.

Like him, she enjoyed special privileges that should have enriched her life but only ever seemed to mock at it. Like him, she had lost a precious gift, the simple joy of being alive. Since being chosen –

more for her beauty than her high birth, Ludovico, for all his faults, being somewhat romantically inclined, she had been granted access to the most private, most protected and sanctified of all places on this good earth, the king's inner chambers, the king's bedroom, the king's bed. But though she loved her ruler, she had not found peace there, nor, of late, too many nights of untroubled sleep. With each new day her Lord and master grew increasingly distant and aloof, until she read into his slightest glance, or gesture of the hand, or raising of an eyebrow, the confirmation of his terminal disdain for her. Above all she missed her companion and confidant, and though the little monk was an unlikely substitute for a king, still she was hungry for an ear into which she could pour her troubles, and that was a service Dromo was only too happy to provide.

"You know the ways of love, Dromo. Tell me, what am I to do?"

"Love, my Lady? No. All I know of anything in this life is between the walls of my cell."

Her chiding look was more affectionate than angry.

"You forget I heard you cry out for your Margery. I thought we had no secrets, you and I."

But the little monk could only shake his head, having no recollection of either the dream or the lady in question. Agnetta had suggested to him, when they first spoke of it, that if indeed he had no recollection of this person, then perhaps the dream was referencing a past life. But Dromo preferred to think it was simply a hallucinatory vision, a gift from his poisoned belly to his fevered brain. Still, it was no surprise that he had dreamed about earthly passions. Since *Fabula* was so near, yet so far out of reach in the throne room, the stories within its pages seemed more real to him than ever before.

"A potion."

It came to him in a flash. She had distracted poor, doomed Alfredo by asking his advice on love.

"A love potion, my Lady. Suppose we actually give the king what you only pretended to want for him … before."

She scoffed.

"Is there such a thing? If so I have never heard of it. Oh, plenty will swear that they know of a recipe, but do any of them actually work?"

It was true. Poisons were far more readily come by than love potions, and their effectiveness always so much easier to gauge. But Dromo was excited by this challenge, and saw in it a way to please both his master and his mistress at one and the same time.

"I will investigate. Of course our…" He paused. For a brief moment even to contemplate such a plan seemed treasonous. But the potential gain surely outweighed any risk.

"… our victim must not be alerted to the deception."

"No. That would never do."

---oOo---

Agnetta had fallen in step with the plan almost at once. She and Dromo went about their task like two children released from drudgery at the end of a long day. The freedom that their close association with the king afforded them meant they could roam freely about the castle. Dromo introduced his new playmate to the kitchen, urging her to pay no heed to the cooks and their minions moving back and forth with pans of hot broth, steaming bowls of porridge or baskets of screeching, squawking chickens for the pot. No one would dare question their giggling presence at the great oak table, pouring milk or cream from a jug, grinding and blending spices in a mortar, tasting, adding a pinch here and a peck there until the mixture was deemed good enough to be tried out on the king. They blended cardamom and ginger root with milk, sweetened the liquor with honey, threw all out and began again. They boiled and simmered, drained and filtered and distilled to arrive at an essence. Dromo elected himself chief sampler of the end products, having no idea what an aphrodisiac should taste like yet still greatly enjoying himself. What innocent pleasure there was in sharing this adventure with another human, especially one so warm, so alive, as Agnetta.

At night, for several days thereafter, the king's consort would present to him the fruits of their labours, a beverage in his own personal flagon that was sometimes hot, sometimes cold, sometimes sweet and sometimes savoury. She made no mention of her pact with Dromo, but sought to give the impression that she had made these drinks herself. She called them remedies, and was grateful when he did not question what they were intended to remedy. This, she told herself, was evidence of his love for her, and his deep understanding that what she did, she also did out of love. He had only temporarily misplaced his humour and would be happy to have it restored by any means, but particularly by having a bedtime drink delivered to him by his faithful and most loyal companion.

Studying Dromo's book by candlelight, as was his nightly practice, he would receive the drink without a word. It would be placed there by his side, at which point the Lady Agnetta would respectfully retire to her bed. In the morning she would see that the flagon had been drained, and she would take it to her co-conspirator to be replenished with some new concoction. Ludovico would not comment, but this she understood to be because the new peace treaty with his enemies had given the king much pause.

On the evening of the fifth day, when the Lady Agnetta arrived at the king's bedchamber with an infusion of dried red berries from a local plant known for its effectiveness as an aphrodisiac, into which some highly flavoured Metagorian honey had been lovingly stirred, she was apprehended by guards and thrown into the castle's deepest dungeon.

---oOo---

"You still seem worried, Ludo."

The throne room was cold, as was every room in the castle, which had turned gradually from stone to ice, then to lead, solid and impenetrable. The great logs that crackled and roared in the fireplace, throwing showers of sparks into the blackness above, barely penetrated its frigid gloom. Ludovico wrapped his robes tightly around himself and shook his head with a weak smile.

"Not worried. Not at all."

You couldn't let them know what you were really thinking. These Szarks made it a rule to smile when they were angry, or stamp their feet when about to make some jest. It would be wise, if you dealt with them, to adopt the same techniques, or you would be lost. The Emperor Gascon seemed not to notice the cold. Perhaps it was his unruly thatch of red hair that kept him warm. They were alone in the room, in conference, and their breath froze in the air as they spoke.

"I'm not worried," Ludovico continued, and was immediately aware that by repeating himself he had already invalidated the statement. "Only one little thing. A trifle..."

"And what might that be?"

"A hunting party of ours, on returning last evening, made mention of some militia, Szark apparently, but many hundreds of armed men, gathered in a valley not three miles from Boroglass. Do you know of this?"

Gascon threw back his head and roared with laughter.

"Do I know of it?" He was almost bellowing, his large belly visibly jiggling beneath the ornate tunic.

"I am only Emperor. Nobody tells me anything."

There was a pause, after which Gascon sighed heavily and raised his eyes to Heaven, cutting through Ludovico's confusion by use of the handy device, employed by all bullies everywhere, of speaking to his new partner as though he were a mewling infant.

"Manoeuvres, my Lord. What have we been talking about? This new peace of ours is precious. It will need protecting."

"Protecting from whom...? If we truly are at peace with the Mendicans..."

Gascon brushed his comment away angrily.

"For shame. We must be ever vigilant. You know this as well as I. No disrespect intended, Ludo, but you must leave these matters to my ... more experienced judgement. Yes, we are all at peace. But I hardly need say to you that a Mendican, after all, is a Mendican."

And a Szark is a Szark, thought Ludovico, but said nothing.

"Actually I am proud that your hunting party stumbled upon our preparations. I was going to reveal them to you myself but ah ... well, I am a modest man, as you know."

For the last hour they had been discussing various fine details of the peace treaty, how best to trade the resources of their three nations for the benefit of all, but by this time Ludovico felt that if he were to suffer one more instant of Gascon's pompous, self-congratulatory bombast, he would lose his mind for good. How he hated this malignant dance, this interplay of false praise and stern reprimand. As for the insistence on addressing him as 'Ludo' …

"But I think we have concluded our business, have we not?"

Now Gascon smiled warmly. Whenever he did so, he appeared to Ludovico at his most evil.

"I had intended to ride out tonight, but the weather looks set to worsen. If you could accommodate my small retinue until the morning, and we will be gone."

"Of course Emperor, my rooms are at your disposal."

Beneath the smile and his expansive gesture, Ludovico seethed with self-loathing. Why had he declined Gustav's offer to obliterate the Szark nation? Yes, the bloodshed on such a large scale would have been regrettable, but it might well have been all over by now, and the guilty parties repenting at their leisure. Gustav of Mendica was not so bad as had been made out. The man was actually quite personable. At least you knew where you were with Gustav. Why had he ever listened to that meddling monk?

No sooner had the thought crossed his mind than Dromo burst into the room, unescorted, almost bumping into Gascon as he was leaving. He was out of breath and red in the face. Ludovico had never seen him this way, and snapped angrily at him.

"What do you want?"

Dromo struggled to control his breathing. He paused and bowed to the departing Gascon of Szark. The Emperor was clearly displeased at such rudeness but nodded curtly to Ludovico before walking swiftly away toward his chambers. At last Dromo found his voice.

"The Lady Agnetta... she has been imprisoned? Why, my Lord? Why would you do such a thing?"

Ludovico's wrath surprised even himself. He rounded on Dromo with such force that the little monk lost his balance and fell to the floor.

"And what right do you have to question my decisions? What are you, but a worthless scribe? Worse still, a prisoner and a murderer. Never forget, Dromo, that I am the one who pardoned you, and I can un-pardon you on a whim."

"Yes, Sire, but please, if you will just hear me..."

"Guards!"

Ludovico clapped his hands twice and the armed guards rushed in, making straight for Dromo. His voice took on the low edge of panic.

"Sire, if you let me explain, I fear you are mistaken as to the nature of my Lady's actions. It was my idea."

The guards had a hold of him and were about to drag him away, but Ludovico was intrigued now.

"Let him be."

Dromo was hauled to his feet and the guards departed with a nod from Ludovico. When the door was firmly shut he reached into the folds of his robe and produced a small leather pouch. He threw it to Dromo.

"What was your idea? This?"

Dromo looked at the king, wide-eyed. He pulled at the drawstring and released a small bundle of dried leaves onto the hexagonal stones of the throne room floor.

"You don't recognise it? It is wolfsbane, sometimes known, appropriately I think, as monkshood. Is this what you intended to kill me with?"

"Sire, no. ... Please."

Ludovico drew a short sword.

"The poison was found among the Lady Agnetta's belongings. I became suspicious when she brought me drinks at night. I poured them all away of course, or I would not be standing here before you. Now tell me the truth, monk, or I will stretch it out of you on that rack you so admire. Were you part of the plan to assassinate me? Who are you working for? Szark or Mendican?"

He held the sword with a less than gentle caress at Dromo's throat.

"Sire, that poison was intended for me. The drinks she served you, they were... potions of another kind. Love potions, Sire."

Ludovico laughed contemptuously, and pressed a little harder with the sword. Dromo's words tumbled from him, as though they might be his last.

"I myself fell ill after the smallest dose of the poison. If not for my manservant, Alfredo, who gorged on it, I would be dead now."

Dromo's pleading was not for himself so much as the Lady Agnetta, for whom his fondness had grown immeasurably since he had forgiven her for Alfredo.

"Love potions. You truly expect me to believe this?"

Dromo nodded furiously. Ludovico's lip curled, but he slowly lowered the sword.

"Tell me everything. From the beginning."

And Dromo poured out the truth, about how Agnetta had hated

him for taking up so much of Ludovico's time that he had neglected her. About how she had had a change of heart after Alfredo's death, about their talks together and their subsequent plan to find a recipe that would rekindle Ludovico's passion.

"Sire, I ask nothing for myself, only that you spare my Lady. A king may become distracted by the weight of his duty, and perhaps, if I may make so bold, forget the one who loves and honours him the most."

Ludovico sheathed his sword and slumped backwards into his throne, dismissing Dromo with a wave of his hand towards the mighty oak doors. Sensing that further argument would not be fruitful, Dromo stood and left with a small bow.

There Ludovico sat, ruminating hour upon hour, until the fire died down. He was too wrapped in his thoughts to feel the cold now. Somewhere in the castle, the Emperor Gascon slept soundly. Elsewhere he knew his consort and former confidante Agnetta would be weeping. And now this monk with his fabulous story, one that if his consort was to be asked he would surely find repeated to him, word for word. Who to believe? If the grinning Szark Emperor was false – and he surely was most of the time, he could have planted either of these people in the castle to act as spies. Ludovico could trust no one now, least of all those whom he loved, or had loved.

Outside the wind howled and a fresh burst of snow fell, so thick and silent as to bury the castle, and the town of Boroglass, and all of Metagoria once and for all. It was gone midnight when Ludovico made his way slowly to the south side of the castle, through the dimly lit corridors to the base of the spiral staircase. He climbed slowly upwards then finally pushed open the door to Dromo's cell. He found the little monk awake and looking terrified. He spoke with a voice as cold as any winter night, as hollow as a wolf's howl.

"I want you to prepare something for me, or at least supervise its construction. I want a coffin. It should be ornate and lined with silk. I want it to be beautiful. I don't care how you do it, but I want it now. I need it for the morrow."

Dromo stared at his sovereign in disbelief. Before leaving Ludovico added dryly...

"... It must be fit for a queen."

---oOo---

Wanting nothing but the petting hand of friendship, possessing nothing but the straggly fur that guarded him against the cold, Sibunan made a perfect companion for Palini. He did not judge him for his past mistakes, nor have a single expectation of his master, save that he be fed a scrap of food when it was available, and even then he would not press for it, but wait patiently, ears cocked, intermittently licking his lips with a loud smacking of jowls. If, as rarely happened, the food was withheld, he would not fret but merely yawn, stretch and go back to sleep.

These were the hardest of hard times, and Palini's gratitude for the dog's presence in his life was beyond measure. They had travelled for days through a mountainous region on the outskirts of Metagoria, weary for lack of food, stumbling blind for want of a star to guide them, the task of covering their tracks made so much harder when two feet and four paws were creating them. What use would it be to try? The Mendican savage on his trail would not be outwitted, and whatever else he accomplished in his desolate and shameful life, Palini would not abandon his canine friend. Besides not eating, they were starved of sleep, stopping only when Palini could go no further, and then only for brief spells, when man and beast would huddle together in the base of a hollow tree for warmth.

And with every step he cursed himself. What good had his experiments with free will done him? They had brought him here, to this desolate place where he was shortly to die, frozen to the bone. He had learned nothing of himself in these past five moons save his capacity to kill his fellow men, or by inaction allow them to die. Was free will, perhaps, something reserved for better, wiser men than he? Was he, Palini, in the end not fit to wield such power? He thought back to his life before meeting the bogus Duc de Pomerance and listening to his lies. He may not have been content with his lot back then, but he had known himself at least to be a servant of God, with his place in Heaven assured. Now he was outcast. Was this his destiny after all? Must it always have turned out this way? If he had not stopped to share his supper, would he still have found himself starving in this snowbound wilderness?

A wisp of smoke was just barely visible against the backdrop of snow-laden trees and a sky as white as parchment, but it spelled hope for the man who emerged from the forest slopes with his faithful hound in tow. The door to the log cabin was wedged shut with a fresh fall of snow. Palini slumped against it, too weak to knock with his frozen fist, and the weight of his body, combined with the snowfall, pushed the door inwards. He collapsed inside, clawing his way across the dusty floor to where a wood fire burned, the first glimmer of warmth and life that he had seen in many a day. Once again he found himself lying prostrate before a fire in worshipful gratitude for its healing flames and he fell into a deep sleep, Sibunan curled obediently by his side.

He would have slept there for several days had not the smell of food cooking on the fire awoken his senses. An old woman was tending the ancient iron pot, in which the carcass of some game bird was slowly broiling. There were some root vegetables and wild herbs in there, too, and the aroma of the resulting soup was like a magical elixir, filling Palini with a longing for his own home and hearth, if it had ever existed, so far distant in space and time. He could not speak as the woman ladled some soup into a bowl, for fear that this was nothing but a dying man's dream and he was really lying half-buried in the snow, as stiff as a ship's mast. But the hot broth gradually soaked into his bones, driving out the cold and restoring his heartbeat to something like its normal rhythm. Then all he could do was nod politely as the old woman went about her business, needing neither conversation nor explanation. He offered Sibu some scraps of meat, but the dog barely raised his head. Then, having finished his meal, Palini slept once more. When he awoke the wizard was there, watching him.

"Aha…" the wizard said, acknowledging his guest.

That he was a wizard, there could be no doubt. The old man had a long, white beard and sported a cloth hat ringed with the skulls of tiny creatures, perhaps birds. Around his neck there were strings of beads and an amulet comprised a strange hieroglyphic carved into a wooden disc. From his shoulders hung a robe that dragged along the floor when he walked, which he did with the aid of a gnarled stick fashioned from a tree branch. Palini suspected that the old woman was his wife, but didn't dare to ask. Something about the wizard's inquisitive stare unnerved him.

"Who are you?"

"My name is Palini."

The wizard produced a pipe, and scraped at its bowl to remove the ashes of his last smoke.

"And what do you call him?" His voice had a rasping, dry quality. He pointed with his pipe-stem at Sibu, still sleeping.

"Sibunan," said Palini.

"Aha…"

"I thank you for your hospitality. I have nothing to give you in return but my labour."

"Nothing?" said the wizard, and he opened his hand to reveal a coin. Palini realised at once that it was the one he had tried to give to Friar Benjamin, the one the friar had given back to him, and the memory triggered such emotion in him that tears sprang unbidden to his eyes. The wizard gave a kind smile and pressed the coin into Palini's palm. Palini was in no position to refuse it.

"You are dressed as a holy man, but you are not a holy man."

"I'm a soldier." Palini then added, a little shamefaced, "How did you know?"

Now at last the wizard gave a smile, and a knowing shrug. He pointed a bony finger at Palini's equally bony, now blooded knees, protruding from beneath the skirt that was his habit.

"If a man be too poor to dress as well as a monk, that is poverty indeed."

There was no malice in the old man's tone. But his look told Palini that he was awaiting an explanation.

"I was set upon. I am travelling… to Szark."

Palini made to move, but collapsed back onto the ground. There

SIX MOONS

was no sense in lying to this man.

"I am travelling to nowhere. I am lost. This coin is all I have in the world. I am a beggar, and I am a sinner. I beseech you, do not squander your generosity upon one such as I. If I can be allowed to gather my strength I will be on my way."

The wizard continued in his calm, measured delivery, sounding like the most ancient of oracles. He took some tobacco from a pouch at his waist and began to fill his pipe.

"From Szark, you say? That is a very long ride from here. And you have no horse."

"I am not from there. At least, I do not pay allegiance to the Emperor. Not any longer."

"Then where are you from?"

"Originally? From Boroglass. I am Metagorian."

"You have family here?"

"My parents are dead. At least …"

He broke off. The effort of remembering weighed heavily.

"… I never knew my real parents. A couple took me in. They found me wandering as a child, abandoned."

"And you are wandering still," said the wizard with a sigh.

The old man bent to the fire, picked up some metal tongs and scooped up a glowing ember. He touched it to the bowl of his pipe and drew smoke into his lungs. Then he returned the ember to the hungry flames. For a moment or two he regarded Palini with a quizzical expression.

"A beggar you may be, a sinner I have no doubt, but you are not lost."

"I am not? Why do you say so?"

185

"Boroglass is nearby."

Palini could only stare at the wizard in disbelief.

"Half a day's walk from here is the town of Boroglass with its castle, seat of the King of Metagoria. It would seem that you have come home, Palini."

---oOo---

Ludovico and the Emperor Gascon had dined together in the banqueting hall along with various members of the court and a small number of visiting dignitaries. A great amount of food and wine had been consumed and Gascon had entertained the assembled company with lurid tales of his personal heroism, though his daring exploits had tended to grow less plausible with each flagon of wine that was drunk. Ludovico found the Szark leader insufferable but kept his temper in check and smiled politely throughout the meal.

Beneath the smile he was in torment. As ever he was weighed down by a decision which he knew could not wait, and it concerned the Lady Agnetta. Scarcely aware of Gascon's boasting, he kept turning the events of the day over in his mind. Dromo's explanation, that Agnetta had not been trying to kill him, but instead woo him, sounded too fantastic in the light of his discovery of the wolf's bane. On the other hand, he had never before had cause to doubt the little monk, who had been most effective as his armourer, even suggesting changes to the design of the cannons that had greatly improved their aim and efficiency. Could he trust his learned advisor? Could he trust the Lady Agnetta? She had already protested her innocence, as she was dragged away to the dungeon, but who wouldn't do the same in such circumstances? For all he knew his mistress was a Szark, or perhaps a Mendican, planted there, awaiting the perfect moment to betray or indeed murder him.

Doubts piled upon doubts in Ludovico's fevered mind to the point where he felt he might lose his senses altogether, but as the evening wore on he came at last to a decision. He would sooner cut his own heart out than do what he knew had to be done, but he also knew that a king must be a king. When the company finally dispersed he and his russet-haired guest took leave of one another, each retiring to their separate quarters. Ludovico knelt by his now empty bed and said a silent prayer, asking God's forgiveness for the deed he was about to commit. He then made his way to Gascon's chamber, walking quickly so as to get there before he changed his mind. Stopping only to instruct two guards to meet him in the dungeons, he then knocked on Gascon's door, declaring his presence in a firm voice that nevertheless betrayed his frail and tenuous disposition. A bewildered and very drunk Emperor opened the door to him.

"My Lord...? Are you ill?"

Ludovico did indeed look unwell, pale and desperately burdened. He almost wept as he pleaded admittance to Gascon's room.

"Emperor, I must speak with you on a matter of some urgency."

"Of course."

Ludovico sat on the edge of Gascon's bed while the Emperor put on his robe.

"I scarcely know where to begin."

"At the beginning, Ludo. I am your servant. If it concerns the peace treaty, I can assure you..."

"No," Ludovico interrupted him, "it is a... more delicate matter. A more… personal matter."

Gascon sat opposite the King of Metagoria and listened while he unburdened himself of his troubles, all of which tumbled from him with the force of a landslide. Ludovico left nothing to the imagination. He and Agnetta had been in love. He had promised to make her his queen but now he had ample cause to doubt her. He could not accept the explanation given by Dromo, that the poison was never intended for him, and was now quite set on his course. All the while as Ludovico spoke, his voice quivering with emotion, Gascon waited respectfully, occasionally nodding in agreement, his brows dancing, now with consternation, now with surprise. When Ludovico was finally spent Gascon gave a deep sigh and looked at the king with genuine pity in his eyes. His voice when he spoke was even and kindly in tone.

"You have my deepest sympathy. It is regrettably true, from what you have told me that there is no other option: she must pay the ultimate price. We Szarks have only one penalty for treason, and you and I both know the Mendicans' position on these matters."

Ludovico's reply was beyond weary.

"We Metagorians are no different, Emperor. Whatever has come between our nations in the past, this much we have always agreed upon. The penalty for treason is death."

There was a pause, a vacuum that Ludovico seemed in no hurry to fill. Gascon seemed genuinely moved but could not help but yawn, as the hour was so late.

"My dear Ludo, as you seem to be resolved…"

"You don't understand," Ludovico blurted out the words. "I cannot see her hang, nor undone by the executioner's axe. I cannot. It would be too much."

"What then...?"

"I would do it with my bare hands. If... If I could..."

He cast around the room in desperation as if looking for an exit. His imploring look finally settled on Gascon, who slowly came to understand what was being asked of him.

"Where is my Lady now?"

Ludovico on impulse reached out to Gascon as if to touch his robe, but as quickly drew back in shame and confusion.

"The dungeons. But... no one must know."

Gascon was sober now, and for the first time spoke with a cool military bearing.

"Take me to the dungeons."

"Are you sure, Gascon?"

"It will be an honour to serve you, my Lord."

And he bowed.

---oOo---

Moments later, the two kings were standing outside one of the dungeons in the bowels of the castle, their faces barely lit by the flickering torch that was fastened to a nearby wall. Ludovico had the key to the cell about his person but his nerves seemed to fail him as he fumbled for it, so much so that Gascon had to reach out a hand to steady him.

"Be brave, my Lord. Your suffering will be over soon. I guarantee it."

Ludovico turned the key in the lock, then paused. With a great effort he steadied his voice, looking Gascon squarely in the eyes, and exhaled slowly.

"Tell me, Emperor," he sighed, "how do you tell truth from falsehood?"

This amused Gascon greatly. There was enormous pride in his answer.

"Simple. I assume that all men lie and act accordingly. Why do you ask?"

"No reason." Then, swiftly, "Let's get it over with."

Ludovico pushed on the door that creaked on its hinges as it slowly opened. Then he ushered his guest into the shadowy recesses of the dungeon. As Gascon's eyes gradually became accustomed to the dark he assumed a puzzled look. There was no sign of any prisoner, let alone the king's consort, the best part of the cramped room being taken up by a long, wooden bench festooned with heavy chains and fitted with large, barrel-like rollers at each end. For a moment Gascon struggled to make sense of what he was seeing, then he smiled broadly.

"It's a rack. I understand now. You intend to stretch the Lady Agnetta, to see if she is false."

"No, my Lord."

Two Metagorian guards swiftly filed into the room and shut the door behind them. Ludovico's voice took on a new quality, as cold and calculating as Gascon's had been.

"I need to ask you some questions concerning the peace treaty."

Gascon was about to laugh then checked himself. It was the first time Ludovico had ever seen the Emperor look doubtful.

"What is the meaning of this?"

"I need to hear the truth."

Outraged, Gascon cried out as the guards seized him, but even as he did so, he knew that his own guards would never hear him this far from their quarters. In his eagerness to despatch the king's consort he had come down here without them. Ludovico had played him at his own game, and won.

"This won't take long," said Ludovico.

Gascon was quickly overpowered.

"I hate to do this to you, Emperor."

Ludovico smiled now, and as Gascon was being forcibly strapped to the device it occurred to him in his anguished state that one of the king's last two statements might not have been true.

---oOo---

Palini had rested by the wizard's fire and its soft glow had rekindled his appetite if not his spirit. The wizard brought cheese with bread and olives, which Palini ate as hungrily as a newborn child at his mother's breast. The meal was concluded with a scoop of wild honey that tasted of the grasslands, hills and valleys of Metagoria. So he had come home, as the wizard said. But home to what, he could not say. In truth he wished for nothing but an end to his odyssey and could not imagine any resolution to it other than at the hands of his pursuers.

His one wish was for the old man and his wife to be spared the same fate, and with this in mind he thanked them both and prepared to step out into the snowy wilderness. He would not run but actively seek out the Mendicans. With luck they would show mercy and execute him at once, foregoing torture. It would be futile to argue that he had not killed his fellow Szark, or rather their fellow Mendican Pietro de Fey, and even if he did defend himself, what of poor Bassett and his brother Geraint? Who would speak for them? What of Friar Benjamin and – for all he knew – Friar Benedict and the rest of the brotherhood? Who would atone for their deaths if not Palini? He deserved to die and could not imagine why he had ever thought to escape his fate. Running was for those who, like the Janus-faced Edouard Apery, imagined they possessed free will.

There remained only one dilemma to resolve. Palini had intended to plead the case for Sibu, his companion and only friend that he realised he must now leave behind. Perhaps if these kindly old folks could see their way to looking after him, they would find in him the love and faithfulness that Palini had so depended on these last few weeks. But when he returned to the fire, to the spot where Sibu had apparently taken up residence, he found the dog was still sleeping. Worse still he could scarce be woken, and when Palini tried gently shaking him, he emitted a pitiful whine as though he had been physically struck. He could not seem to raise his head and his eyes, when Palini peeled back one of the lids, had taken on a milky, glazed appearance.

No worse punishment could there be than to see this animal suffer. Palini was in despair. He broke down in tears and could not be consoled. The old woman crossed herself to see the violence of his grief. Finally the wizard intervened.

"I have some herbs which may be of help."

Palini watched, mute, as the wizard laid his hands on Sibu's fur. The dog whimpered but did not resist as he examined its stomach and stroked its muzzle. Palini, his bloodshot eyes bulging from their sockets, sensed the old man's kindly intentions and relaxed a little.

"Anything. Just do what you can."

"Aha…" the wizard said softly, "Aha…"

The small hut became a temple as the wizard went about his business. The smell of incense filled the air and the old woman muttered an incantation under her breath. A wooden bowl was procured and various dried herbs were sprinkled into it. Mixed with water they were formed into a paste that was then applied to Sibu's gums. The wizard worked slowly and calmly, his every action measured and discrete so that his administering to his patient became a ritualistic dance. This had the effect of further soothing Palini. And all the time the wizard spoke to Sibu, calling him by name, evoking ancient spirits.

"Aha… Sibunan is a dog-god, a dog-god as in 'Anubis'. Aha…"

Palini could not decipher his words but it hardly mattered. They had the effect of placing him in a trance state where all cares and all fears were subsumed in a feeling of grace and well-being. The treatment continued for several hours, or perhaps days. Palini could not have told the difference – then at the end of it all, Sibu passed quietly into the next world.

"It is over," said the wizard, seemingly quite satisfied with the outcome of his labours.

Palini stared open-mouthed for a moment then, trembling, flew into a rage, flailing his arms in such a pitch of frenzy that he knocked the wizard's hat from his head. Wisps of the old man's thinning hair flew up like white horns. The old woman screamed and the wizard crouched down, raising his arms in a feeble effort to protect himself. Accusations spewed from Palini.

"Liar! Demon! What of your herbs!? Your prayers!?"

"What of them?" the wizard croaked.

"They were supposed to cure him."

The wizard spoke quickly, moving instinctively to distance himself from the verbal onslaught.

"Not to cure him, to ease his passage. The ritual was for you, as well as Sibunan. There was no other way to help you both."

Palini kicked the cooking pot from its perch, spilling its contents across the floor, then looked around for some other object to smash or bring down upon his enemy. Furious as he was, however, he could not continue his assault on one so old. Tears of frustration and sorrow flowed down his cheeks and he slumped to the ground, utterly defeated. The wizard sensed that the storm was passing and his voice softened.

"He has gone to a better place."

"I should send you to join him. You killed my dog! My Sibu!"

"With herbs and prayers? No. His time had come."

Palini wept openly, laying a despairing hand on Sibunan's fur. The wizard tried to reassure him once again.

"The ancients believed that after death ..."

"... we live our life over. Yes... I know about the ancients. I know about destiny. It cannot be changed."

Palini stared hard at the wizard, wanting answers but expecting none. His remark went unchallenged, and he fell to contemplating his own desperate, accursed fate. Then, after a little while he spoke quietly, his words sounding like echoes from distant canyons.

"I lived according to God's will. All I knew was poverty. So I took my life in my own hands, living instead by my wits."

"Did it cure you of your poverty?"

There was a pause as Palini weighed his answer.

"Yes. But it brought me misery."

"Aha…"

"It brought me here. So how has my destiny been changed? I was born to suffer. Free will is an illusion."

The wizard regarded Palini with eyes as old as time. If it were true what the ancients said, then he had lived many lives.

"Your journey is not yet over. Perhaps you will find peace here in Boroglass."

Palini wiped a sleeve across his tear-stained face, his sorrow now eclipsed by anger. He grimaced with disdain at the old man's words of comfort.

"Why? Is this a special place? Is there magic here?"

"Of course."

"And why is that?"

"Because, Palini, there is magic everywhere. Everything is magic."

---oOo---

The coffin was almost finished. Dromo had supervised every element of its design and construction with the greatest pleasure, and fancied that the project had almost restored him to his former state of grace. The whole night he had toiled away, delegating tasks to his small but dedicated team of carpenters, and all the while displaying, for him, a most uncharacteristic good humour. He stopped work only to satisfy the demands of his ever-expanding waistline, so that the floor of the workshop had become littered with lamb bones, apple cores and peach stones.

Now, stepping back, he felt more than satisfied with the finished article. Under his supervision what had been the crudest of wooden boxes was now transformed into a casket fit for a queen, just as Ludovico had requested. The edges of the box had been adorned with decorative bronze curlicues, and along the sides there were ornamental diamond-shaped studs. The whole had been stained and polished to a high lustre, and though there had not been time for any elaborate carvings, still Dromo felt that he had created the desired effect. A king's consort could be buried in such a box.

It was just before dawn when Ludovico entered the room to inspect the work.

"You have excelled yourself, armourer."

"Thank you, my Lord."

"Where are the air holes? Did you remember?"

"Yes, Sire. They are hidden along the sides."

Ludovico looked closer at the diamond studs and smiled when he saw that they were actually raised on tiny metal legs that had been curled around so as to be out of sight, then fastened to the wood. Behind each stud was a small, round hole that could barely be detected from a casual glance at the coffin. Ludovico clearly approved, giving Dromo a pat on the shoulder. It was the first time that he had ever shown affection to the little monk, and Dromo felt moved.

"Was the …apparatus effective?"

Ludovico nodded gravely.

"Gascon was to give a signal from the battlements to the waiting Szark and Mendican armies."

"We will be ready for them, my Lord."

"Do not doubt that we are greatly outnumbered. But we have the hand cannons. Your new design works well. They will sound like the wrath of God, and if it be His will, we will prevail."

Dromo had to swallow hard to ask his next question.

"May I … enquire of the Emperor's health, Sire?"

"He is alive, for now. I have one more task I wish him to perform. But it need not concern you, Dromo. Whatever sins you committed in the past, you have atoned for them. You must leave at once."

Dromo was not about to leave the castle under any circumstances. He quickly deflected the question back to his sovereign.

"And what about you, my Lord? You cannot risk being captured."

"Why is that?"

"Metagoria must not fall, Sire. As long as you are alive, there is hope."

The king nodded gratefully.

"I will do my duty."

Before Ludovico could utter another word the door to the workshop swung slowly back and the Lady Agnetta entered in a flowing gown, followed by two solemn courtiers and a priest in ceremonial robes. The king bowed deeply to his mistress, then to the priest. Thinking she had come to inspect her unusual carriage, Dromo prepared to open the coffin and reveal its silk-lined interior, but Ludovico took Agnetta by the hand and they both faced the priest who began to intone sacred words. Dromo was at first confused, then with the deepest feeling of awe he realised what he was witnessing.

This would not be the most splendidly regal of weddings. There was to be no feasting or dancing, no jousting, no elaborate displays of strength or archery skills. No poems to the new queen would be read aloud, or songs sung in her honour. There would be no formal leave-taking of the newly-weds from the festivities to the sanctity of their marriage bed. Instead Queen Agnetta was to make her escape from the castle, not even knowing whether she would see her beloved again.

But she would be his queen, and despite the humble nature of this union, or perhaps because of it, Dromo felt moved to his core. The two lovers exchanged rings and vows, after which the king bowed once more and she responded by curtseying daintily before him. They scarcely had time to seal their bond with a kiss before Ludovico whispered an instruction to one of his intimates and the queen was gently guided away. She paused in the doorway of the room and glanced back at the coffin that had been made ready for her departure, her face betraying neither fear nor anger but only resignation mixed with a certain womanly pride and determination. Dromo thought he had never before seen such a beautiful face. It was a beauty beyond the wonders of science, a beauty that no fictional tale could begin to describe or replicate.

When the bride and groom had left, Dromo fell into a deep reverie. He understood that he was going to die here in this castle on the point of a sword, but that knowledge seemed much easier to bear since he had looked upon the face of beauty. So strange and so powerful was this emotion that it hit him with the force of a thousand lifetimes passed, and a thousand yet to come.

---oOo---

The fact that he had a rival came as no surprise. Being so stricken in love, there was only one thing that could have surprised him, and that would be if no one else could see what was so plain to see, that the object of his affection was divine. The detestable boy went by the name of Randolph and he was, like Margery, a thing of beauty. At least that's how it seemed to Palini in his deranged and overheated state. Where Palini was thin and gaunt, Randolph was neatly proportioned, athletic and muscular. Where Palini was tongue-tied, Randolph was verbose and charming. Worst of all, where Palini was as poor as a field mouse, Randolph was the son of a moderately wealthy landowner. Every bit as much as he silently worshipped his beloved, Palini hated and despised her principle suitor.

He was a strutting cockscomb, a popinjay. That much was clear to everyone except Margery. Palini read into her every response to Randolph's advances the most immodest exuberance. Each time she skipped and fawned in Randolph's presence with wanton abandon, playing the coquette for him, Palini's ravaged heart was pierced anew. He would have hated her if he did not love her. He would have choked her with his bare hands if every fibre and tissue of his being did not cry out to protect and cherish her unto the end of his days.

There was a festive spirit abroad in the village and every youth and farmhand, as well as every maiden, was expected to attend a dance that night. It was a solstice, a time when fertility was celebrated, and even this conspired to further torture poor, lovelorn Palini. Tonight there would be dark couplings and an end to fevered longings for the lucky ones. There would be whispered endearments, sweet caresses and secret rendezvous. Love tokens would be exchanged. Palini had been in receipt of the same on previous occasions, but they had only ever moved him to a sense of his own worth, which sensation would quickly fade as the fun of the chase slowly withered on the vine.

Now he realised the stakes had been raised, and so highly did he value the prize that he found himself loath to even enter the arena, and wished that for just this one night he could be somewhere else, or someone else. He took an age to prepare himself, though he only had one set of clothes, and several times he set out for the dance, only to return home cursing his cowardice and indecision.

He arrived late in a cold sweat, already exhausted from his jealousy and anger before the festivities had even begun, but the elaborate plans he had made to show indifference to Margery and the rest of her female accomplices were immediately quashed as the young lady of his dreams sought him out, appearing suddenly at his side and taking him by the arm. This time she was not robed in mill dust but in the prettiest of summer dresses. No mere baker's daughter now but the rarest, loveliest flower of womanhood.

"Where have you been? I need you. Come with me."

His legs, though unsteady, could not move. His arms hung like lead at his sides. He went to speak but his jaw was slack, clogged by a tongue that seemed suddenly to have outgrown his mouth. She giggled.

"Don't look at me like that. I have my father's horse and cart. I need you to take me to the haybarn at the top of Lindo's farm. You know? The one behind the church?"

He was led away like a drunken puppy, numb to all sensation but the touch of her hand on his arm. But when they rounded a corner of the village square he was greeted by a sight that returned all feeling to his body with the force of a lightning strike. Randolph was lounging in the back of the one-horse cart, propped against a loose bale of straw. He laughed to see the gangly mute she had brought along to be their equerry.

"Are we ready, Margery? Don't keep me waiting."

He held out a hand for the maiden and she climbed up next to him as Palini stared in disbelief. There was a pause when it seemed that he might launch himself bodily at his rival, but still he could not utter a word, nor scarcely breathe. To add insult, Margery and Randolph seemed to be enjoying his confusion. Margery made a face to show just how annoyed she was at his impertinence.

"Don't stand there staring. The field behind the church, Palini. Are you hard of hearing? What's the matter with you?"

Despite his every impulse to turn away, strike out at someone or burst into tears, Palini was under the spell of her golden voice, like water over pebbles, and to his amazement he found himself slowly climbing up into the driver's seat and taking the reins. The horse moved off at a leisurely pace and his humiliation was complete.

Halfway to their destination the lane was crossed by a large oak. One of its branches leaned at a low angle across the lane, forcing Palini to duck his head. His passengers had been silent up to now, and he fancied he could feel their eyes watching him, feel them grinning together at his helpless obedience. He hoped the thick branch would decapitate Randolph and to that end would have steered the cart straight into it, except that he could not risk harming his beloved. But no sooner had the thought occurred to him than the boy Randolph, rather than ducking the branch, leaped up from the cart and hoisted his body effortlessly up into the tree, scampering up it like a squirrel whilst emitting a loud whooping. Palini tugged back on the reins but Margery was suddenly by his side. She whispered in his ear.

"Drive on."

"Drive on, Palini, drive on!" echoed Randolph from his branch.

As the young woman pressed her body against his on the cramped seat, Palini felt a wave of giddiness descend upon him once again. Randolph was still laughing in the tree, though his voice was growing fainter as the nag progressed up the lane and Margery looked straight ahead. When she did speak there was tenderness.

"You are such a hard man to get to know."

"I thought … you and Randolph…"

The giggle came again.

"Randolph does not like girls, though he likes them well enough when they are at play. He likes nothing better than to help them in the execution of a daring and dangerous plot."

She squeezed his arm, flashing him the most enticing, the hungriest of looks. The horse ambled on towards the barn in the field behind the church. Palini exalted in the slow rhythm of its hooves in the dry dust of summer, and knew himself to be as happy as it was possible for any young man to be.

6
MARCH

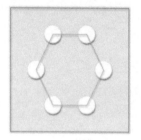

The combined armies of the Szark Empire and the Kingdom of Mendica had met and joined together in a show of strength that had never before been seen in Metagoria. The hills and grasslands surrounding Boroglass bristled with their pikestaffs, banners and flags. Dense forest, now bare of leaves, stood sentinel, as black and foreboding as the massed armies were emblazoned with colour: red for Mendica, gold and blue for Szark. Soon all would be stained red with blood, but for now the infantry of both sides mingled amicably. It is a universal truth that man has no greater love for his fellows than when he stands beside them cheek by jowl on the battlefield. A common enemy is the one thing guaranteed to make the bitterest rivals put down their swords and embrace, weeping upon each other's shoulders.

King Gustav, acting as commander of the forces in the absence of the Emperor Gascon, was positioned on a broad mound within sight of the castle. With him were a dozen or so of his elite Mendican guard, including his lieutenant, Justice. It hardly mattered now that they could be seen from the castle battlements. The Metagorian army garrisoned inside could not hope to defend themselves against an invasion of such magnitude, no matter how bravely they fought and how well they were armed. It only remained for Ludovico to surrender his crown and his nation.

Gascon would, at this very moment, be listing the king's options to him. There were only two: fight and be killed, or surrender and be banished. It had been a point of contention between the two rival kings as to whether Ludovico be allowed to live. Gustav had argued for his execution as a means of bringing about an end to the Metagorian nation state once and for all. Ludovico had no heirs, it was well known. There would be no further claims to his throne and even if there were, a swift and brutal beheading would act as a deterrent to any other family members who might consider following in his footsteps. With typical Szark obstinacy, however, Gascon had argued for showing mercy to the king, and after much heated discussion Gustav had let him have his way. In the unlikely event that Ludovico refused to surrender, a prearranged signal would tell them to attack. If this happened, the battle would be over in a matter of minutes.

A hush descended, and the whole world seemed to hold its breath. Snowflakes began to fall, some as large as autumn leaves. They settled everywhere, lending an unearthly sparkle and glimmer to the landscape. Gustav glanced across at Justice who had a fixed, morose look about him. He raised a mocking eyebrow in his lieutenant's direction.

"How now, Justice? Why so gloomy? Just because a Szark deserter, travelling on foot, managed to outpace you? Perhaps you, too, would have fared better with a hound for a companion?"

The lieutenant acknowledged the taunt with the barest of nods. He could not bring himself to smile for he burned with indignation, but even had he attempted it his battle-scarred features could not have fashioned themselves into anything resembling amusement.

Justice, or Matthew as he had once been known, had earned a face quite different from the one he had been born with, courtesy of the ministrations of inhuman, cold steel upon his once handsome features. It was of no consequence to him that he had influenced the outcome of every battle with his reckless heroism, since winning had only led to more fighting with no end in sight. He barely recognised himself anymore, and he wondered, as he had wondered his whole life, how his heavenly twin would judge him. Luke, watching from his perfect world in the sky, would surely deny him the spoils of war, or the simple satisfaction of pitting himself against another and prevailing. Luke would know that he would lose the fight one day and fall by another's hand, either exhausted from old age or simply overpowered by a warrior as bent on raising hell as he was.

From up here he could see the rooftops of Boroglass stretching away towards the sea, where the masts of the Metagorian fleet were greatly in evidence. Much use would Ludovico's warships be to him now, he thought. Justice had grown up here along the shore, played in and among the squabble of wooden dwellings that comprised the town. In a few short hours the joint forces of the Szark and Mendican alliance would occupy Boroglass, the castle and all of the lands that surrounded it. The Metagorians would be sold into slavery and what buildings deemed of no use would be put to the torch, either as a warning to those who might seek revenge, or simply as recreation and reward for the victorious armies.

Justice felt nothing for these people who had raised him. He was a mercenary, and a soldier. The taking of life was his trade.

Gustav was becoming impatient now. The last thing he wanted, in this biting cold weather, was a long-drawn-out siege. The castle was well fortified and Ludovico would know that he could hold out for several days if necessary, perhaps longer. But what would be the point, against such combined forces? Gascon would surely convince the king of the folly of sitting tight.

"What's keeping him? Why no signal?"

"The sun is low in the sky, Sire, and its light is weak. Perhaps we cannot see his signal."

"Look! There!"

Gustav was pointing at the castle, but not to the battlements as expected. The drawbridge was slowly descending across the castle's moat, the clanking of its heavy chains ringing out starkly against the hush of the white, snow-muffled scene.

"Good. He is surrendering."

It took an age for the drawbridge to come to rest, then a horse and cart appeared, draped in funereal black silks. A lone rider, also in black, sat holding the reins as the cart crossed the drawbridge and slowly moved away from the castle. On the back of the cart was a coffin, sheltered from the snow beneath an elaborately embroidered canopy. Gustav and Justice exchanged glances. This was not part of the plan. Ludovico was not in sight.

"What is this? Some trick?"

Gustav dug his heels in his horse's side, spurring it into life. His knights mounted their steeds to follow but he signalled them to wait.

"Justice. We will meet this."

Justice and King Gustav made their way up the ridge and reined in their horses at a discreet distance from the castle. He raised his hand for the cart to stop. The driver obeyed and Gustav dismounted to inspect his load.

"Where are you bound?"

The man had his hood pulled up about his face against the cold. He said nothing but pointed across to Boroglass, where a church steeple was visible above the tree line and the surrounding dwellings.

Justice answered for him.

"The burial ground is up yonder, Sire."

Gustav turned back to the driver of the cart.

"And who has died, pray? Someone of importance, I fear?"

This time the man spoke up. He was an emaciated, half-starved fellow with a sallow, muddy complexion.

"The Lady Agnetta, consort to King Ludovico."

"How so? What did she die of?"

The driver shrugged. It would be no concern of his. Gustav did not wait for an answer but considered for a moment. The Mendicans were a fiercely superstitious people, with many sacred rites relating to death and the next world. It was very much against their beliefs and practices to open a coffin. This would be a serious insult to the dead and could have equally grave consequences for the living, according to Mendican lore. But if it really was a trick and King Ludovico was inside, Gustav had better do the unthinkable and remove the lid. Despite Emperor Gascon's reservations, it was important that the Metagorian bloodline be curtailed. The king, thus exposed, would rot in a prison cell, and think himself lucky.

Gustav laid a hand on the cart and spoke in a loud voice, conscious that if the body inside were after all a living, breathing soul he would hear every word.

"What do you think, Justice? A favoured consort dies and this, we are expected to believe, is how her king mourns her, with this tawdry and too humble procession?"

"Unless the king himself is inside the coffin, Sire. It would be just like the cowardly Ludovico to attempt to escape his fate, leaving his men, and his consort, behind to die."

"Unthinkable. No ruler could commit such an act of betrayal and still call himself a king."

There was silence. Gustav was aware that his knights were watching him closely. It was vital that he make the right decision. He could not appear weak before the men. Which was the greater risk: that Ludovico was escaping, or that the coffin did actually contain a corpse? If the Lady Agnetta were inside, and alive, it would be of little consequence to let her pass unharmed. But if the casket was opened, and she lay in there decomposing ...

Justice was in no doubt about how they should proceed.

"We must open the casket."

He moved to dismount, but Gustav interjected, signalling to the driver of the cart.

"Move on."

The driver obeyed and took up the reins. But as he did so, it seemed to Gustav that he gave a parting glance in his direction, one that contained more than a hint of satisfaction. The wheels of the cart clattered over cobbled stones as he hurried on towards the cemetery on the hill. The Mendican knights parted for him to continue on his way. To a man they gave the sign of the cross as the coffin passed them. But suddenly Gustav cried out.

"Stop him!"

There was a sudden murmuring of consternation from the assembled knights as the king's intention became apparent. One or two men cried out a warning despite themselves, but a look from Justice immediately silenced them. He had come level with the horse that pulled the cart and now took the reins. The driver, seemingly betraying his fear, could not meet the lieutenant's eye. Justice signalled to four of his elite guard who came forward equally nervously, each man looking to the king to be sure that he approved their actions. Gustav nodded and they climbed aboard the cart. The hush that now descended upon the scene was like the grave itself. Even the horses had ceased their restless stomping and fretting.

On examination of the coffin's ornate design, one of the guards discovered Dromo's handiwork and called across to the lieutenant.

"Breathing-holes!"

Gustav smiled to himself, relieved that he had successfully called Ludovico's bluff. To have made the wrong decision would have jeopardised the coming battle, there could be no doubt, for to open a coffin without due ceremony was, in Mendica at least, worse than blasphemy.

"So. Let's find out who rides to the cemetery this fine day?"

Without pause the four Mendican guards prised open the coffin lid and flung it to the ground. Instantly, a swarm of flies rose up from the casket and headed in all directions. Simultaneously an evil, deathly stench pervaded the whole area. One of the guards gave a guttural cry of horror at what he gazed upon, while another stepped away with such recoil that he tripped and fell backwards over the side of the cart, landing heavily on the snow-covered pebbles below. Justice leaped up to get a better look. He stared down into the coffin. No stranger to death, yet even he had to clamp a hand over his mouth to stifle a yell, and only then, after a second or two, did he find the courage to turn to Gustav, eyes wide, with a desperate shake of the head.

Gustav's face, staring back at the lieutenant, grew almost as white as that belonging to the decomposing corpse in the coffin as it lay there, clad in the pristine white wedding dress in which it was to be buried.

---oOo---

Up above, on the battlements, Dromo was watching the drama unfold. When he had refused to leave the castle Ludovico had respected his decision and did not press him on the point. To push doubts aside he supervised the loading of the new hand cannons whose manufacture he had overseen. There were a dozen of them ranged about the ramparts of the castle, each manned by one soldier to do the firing and two more for reloading. Dromo had seen to it that the bore of each cannon was of spiral design so as to impart a spin on the shot as it left the muzzle of the gun. This would make it fly straighter and with greater accuracy.

Dromo was satisfied that his design would inflict great damage on the invading armies, and though it might not deter them indefinitely, the thundercrack of twelve roaring cannons if fired simultaneously would certainly give them pause for thought. Back in the throne room two moons ago he had predicted what would happen when the unstoppable force met the immovable object: mutual annihilation. Not for his sake but for Ludovico's he now prayed that he was wrong. These castle walls were thick, and they might yet repel the enemy. He was able to peer over them with a little effort.

Down below he could just make out Gustav and his Mendican knights in a confused huddle around the cart and its poisonous cargo. The coffin had been sealed up again, and the cart was now resuming its journey. That would be of little comfort to Gustav of Mendica, so Dromo had been advised. And to prove the point a wave of uneasy movement was sweeping through the gathered throng, so that the soldiers' ranks, formerly so disciplined, now looked suddenly fluid and tenuous. It seemed that Ludovico's plan was working, at least for now. The second and most audacious phase was about to be put into action.

Dromo could do nothing more to affect the outcome of the battle, and indeed a great weariness had come over him, so he issued an order or two, quite unnecessarily, and retired. He made his way slowly back to the sanctuary of his cell. With each available man at his station the castle seemed almost eerily quiet as he hefted his now considerable bulk down the maze of dimly lit corridors, then up the spiral staircase to the top of the tower. Closing the door behind him he sat at the same desk where he had indulged his passions, all those moons ago, passions that he could scarcely recall in the light of all that had happened. Now in place of his beloved books he found a bowl of peaches that he had brought from the kitchen that morning. Their perfume was intoxicating, and he brought one to his mouth, but could not eat. He replaced it in the bowl.

He looked around him at the cramped, cold cell with its dingy walls stained black with rain, white with birds' mess. How could it be that it had once seemed so endlessly engaging, so alive with possibility. Dromo braced himself, for the first time ever, against the certain knowledge that whatever happened on this bitterest of days, his cosy confinement was over.

---oOo---

Just beyond the drawbridge, a phalanx of Metagorian knights hung back, presumably knowing that to attack such a large army was suicide. Instead they seemed to be waiting, and keenly watching events unfold. Gustav was yelling to his troops to stay in line and await his next order. Some of those among the large contingent of Szarks were displaying disdain for their Mendican counterparts, openly laughing at what they saw as the craven superstition on display around them. In the absence of their leader Gascon, those of lower rank, the generals, struggled to bring them to order, and some of the Mendicans were taking great offence at this lack of respect.

Gustav, disgusted at himself for this turn of events, abandoned any idea of waiting for Gascon's signal, preparing to storm the castle right away. But there was another surprise in store.

He and Justice whirled around to see the figure of Ludovico framed by the entrance to the castle, on horseback and in full battledress, helmet and visor above the green of his breastplate. His arm was raised, with sword in hand, and there could be no doubt from his posture that he was not about to surrender.

---o0o---

At this point, edging his way through the throng of soldiers was a tall, gaunt man in a monk's habit that barely covered his bony knees. Palini moved like a sleepwalker, oblivious to all but his desire to get to the castle. With his beloved Sibu now gone, he had no more reason to live, and so nothing more to fear. Why his frail legs had brought him here was a mystery he had no desire to unravel. Perhaps, after all, he had been destined to find his way back to Boroglass all along. He looked up at the moss-covered walls of the Metagorian stronghold with their steadily thickening coat of powdery snow, and realised that every brick and every detail was familiar to him. Here was home, he thought, here he would finally meet his destiny.

But how to enter this magical realm?

Despite the odds he was facing, Ludovico still sat brandishing his sword defiantly on the drawbridge, his sparse retinue of knights in evidence behind him. Gustav laughed aloud at the absurdity of his stance.

"Ludovico," he called out, "do you not see how many of us are assembled here? Has the Emperor not explained the situation to you?"

There was no answer. Ludovico was evidently taunting him, daring him to lead the attack.

"You are holding the Emperor of Szark prisoner, I presume. Bring him out here, and I may spare your life. It was the Emperor who suggested as much. I would have chopped off your head."

Still no answer.

"You are braver than I thought, my Lord. And more foolhardy."

At a signal from Gustav, the advance formations of foot soldiers with pikestaffs angled towards their prey appeared over the crest of the hill, some flying Szark pendants, others Mendican. The sound of their tramping feet as they crushed the new fallen snow echoed menacingly around the castle walls.

Then, perhaps a little unnerved by Ludovico's show of bravery, Gustav suddenly put humour aside in favour of action. He motioned to one of his knights to pass him a weapon. The knight put his hand on the sword hilt at his side but Gustav waved impatiently at him.

"Give me a crossbow."

The bow was summoned up at once, and a bolt loaded. It was handed to Gustav who aimed it at his rival.

"Your last chance to surrender, Ludovico."

When no reply was forthcoming Gustav loosed the bolt. His aim was faultless and it struck the middle of Ludovico's chest, puncturing the metal of his armour with an audible thud. Ludovico twitched violently once and slumped over like a broken marionette. There was a deathly pause and he slipped suddenly from his horse to the ground, one foot still in the stirrup. Instead of coming to his aid his guards pulled back inside the castle, evidently fearing they would be next. The battle was over before it had begun. Gustav dismounted and with Justice by his side he approached the lifeless king. But as he stood gloating over the body of his vanquished foe he noticed something strange. The king still held his arm in the same position, which looked most unnatural now that he was prostrate, lying there on the drawbridge. Justice reached down to prise the sword from the dead man's fingers, then stepped back in alarm.

"Sire, look here."

The sword had been fastened to Ludovico's hand with a winding sheet, which in turn was attached to a wooden staff that held his arm straight, running down inside his armour where it was finally attached to his belt. A familiar gold belt buckle shone out with a yellow light. In one motion Gustav pulled the helmet from the dead man's head and the assembled knights stared down, stupefied, at the flame-red hair, dead eyes and gagged mouth of the Emperor of Szark.

By now several members of the Szark High Command had pushed their way through the Mendican ranks and were approaching on horseback. Many more foot soldiers and pikemen were following on behind. Meanwhile, the Metagorian militia who had formed the bogus king's guard took one look at the massed ranks of Szarks and Mendicans and retreated further into the castle. Some tried frantically to lower the portcullis, but a volley of crossbow bolts drove them back and the great metal gate froze halfway in its downward plunge. The Mendican knights prepared to push forward, but before they could do so there was a great commotion. The Szarks had reached their Emperor's stricken body and a cry went up.

"The Emperor is dead! They have killed Gascon!"

The massed ranks of Mendican and Szark foot soldiers surged forwards as one to ascertain the truth of this. In the confusion one man was impaled on a sword wielded by a soldier wearing opposing insignia, and one of his own instinctively retaliated, mace in hand. The first blood flowed and there was mounting fury on both sides. Gustav was yelling to the Szarks, imploring their attention. He had been tricked by Ludovico but could not make himself heard. His words were drowned out by the howls of protest that mounted in volume as the message that the Emperor was dead got relayed from one group of Szarks to the next. Dead from a crossbow bolt to the heart, and by the hand of Gustav of Mendica!

Palini, still fixated on his mission to get within the castle walls, went wholly unnoticed as fights broke out all around him, Szarks turning on the surprised Mendicans who only moments before had been their staunchest allies. Inevitably, more swords were drawn and a Szark bowman fell to the ground, mortally wounded. This triggered fresh outrage and the fighting spread backwards through the ranks of pikemen, bowmen and cavalry, fanning out in all directions, each drop of blood spilled only adding to the hysteria.

The fighting grew as a fire does from its initial spark to a mighty conflagration. What had seemed like a formidable military machine, drilled and bent to their task, now turned into a boiling sea of conflict. Up above, the Metagorian soldiers stood ready, their cannons loaded, but there was no one to instruct them as to when to fire, or indeed where to aim. No matter. What need of weapons, when their enemies were falling on their own swords?

Embroiled in the conflict, Palini found himself suddenly knocked to the ground as one particularly savage skirmish turned in his direction. Some nameless force, a combination of Szark and Mendican aggression, was thrashing its way across his path and he lay for a moment on the hard ground feeling kicks and blows rain down upon him. The fact that they were not aimed at him did nothing to alleviate his stress. With a great effort he managed to crawl out from beneath the heaving bodies and as he struggled to reorientate himself he caught sight of Gustav and his henchmen with their backs to the castle, slashing with their swords at anyone who approached. Suddenly it seemed a pathway opened up between groups of fighting men and he leaped forward with only seconds to spare before it closed behind him. He ducked under the portcullis and all at once found himself inside the castle.

---oOo---

On a hillside on the outskirts of Boroglass the modest funeral procession came to a halt. The driver of the cart was helped down by two of the king's men who had been waiting there. This man, or rather this lady, now Queen Agnetta, removed her hooded vestment, and the two men bent their knees respectfully. The queen nodded her thanks and they rose to their feet. She had daubed her face with mud and completed the disguise with the rude livery of a servant. She and Ludovico had taken a chance that the Mendican king would not recognise her, since the two had only met once before. Besides, they knew from experience that a king never looked too closely at the face of a man whose earthly mission was to drive a cart. Of course there was a risk that the ruse would be discovered, but Ludovico had reasoned that Gustav would be more interested in the occupant of the casket than in his or her travelling companion. If the funeral cart were to be allowed on its way, the plan would be deemed to have worked well enough, Agnetta being out of harm's way. If, as Ludovico suspected, Gustav sensed he was being tricked, so much the better. He would open the lid, and be damned.

The two men hoisted the coffin from the cart, taking great care with it, as they had been instructed. The grave had already been dug and their two shovels stood at attention nearby. Agnetta looked back down the hill from whence the sounds of combat were drifting up towards them. The carnage showed no sign of abating. Men and horses lay dead or dying. The snow was falling thickly now, forming white pillows that topped the distant castle walls and turrets. It was the strangest of sights, beautiful and ugly at the same time, nature bloody yet serene, strange and incongruous to behold. Nevertheless, the sounds of bloodlust, mingling with the helpless cries and groans of the injured, weighed heavily, and she muttered a silent prayer for her king and her subjects.

The two gravediggers had tied ropes around the coffin and stood ready to lower it. To their surprise, Agnetta gestured for the lid to be removed. They obeyed and once again the air surrounding the coffin buzzed with flies, and was fouled by the unmistakable stench of decaying flesh. If the two men shared the Mendicans' superstition surrounding death, Agnetta did not. She looked almost lovingly, for the last time, at the face of the young boy she had accidentally poisoned. Even in death Alfredo Duschene retained a coolly feminine grace. His features, having been somewhat preserved by the intense cold, had not yet begun to liquefy. He lay dressed in the royal gown, with his lute by his side, his expression unchanged from that which he wore in life. It seemed to say: "It was a pleasure."

The coffin lid was replaced and Alfredo was laid to rest for the second time. Agnetta apologised to the boy for disturbing his rest at the cemetery and said another prayer for his mortal soul. As she did so, she lightly stroked her belly. It was too early to say, but she had the strongest feeling that after nine moons had passed she would be blessed. Whatever happened now, she felt sure, the royal bloodline would endure.

There would be a third Ludovico after all.

---oOo---

Though the castle was full with its complement of military personnel, it was eerily silent, in contrast to the din from outside. Each yeoman was at his post, weapon at the ready, focused and alert, eyes fixed on the enemy without. Even the knights on their snorting chargers held their tongues. Wanting only to live, expecting only to die, they could find no words of comfort for each other and so waited in silence as Palini passed among them.

There was no need to search the castle, for he would not have known what he was searching for, and besides, Palini was at peace. It sufficed that every aspect of the castle's construction, from its mightiest foundation stones to its lofty keep, to the timber frame that held the ceilings aloft and the turrets jutting proudly from each corner, belonged to him. The man whose only possession had been an inability to possess, who had won and lost a wife, as well as two sons, was now a king, possessing all he saw. He ventured deeper into the castle, and none barred his passage.

Two mighty oak doors, standing fully twice his height, revealed themselves. He pushed on one of them and it opened slowly onto a large room, bare but for an ornately carved throne. The walls of the room were bedecked with trophies, royal coats of arms and other ephemera, and the floor at his feet was a honeycomb of six-sided tiles that radiated outwards to every corner. Immediately he felt warm air caressing him. A fire blazed and crackled in an enormous grate, so wide you could have roasted an ox above the logs that seemed to chatter and laugh together as the flames slowly consumed them. Then Palini noticed something.

Up above, perched on a wide stone shelf that ran the full length of the fireplace, was a large book or ledger, of a kind he was acquainted with only by hearsay. It seemed to Palini that the book shone with a light from within, but this he realised might be an illusion, created by the flickering of candles from an imposing six-sided iron girder above. Being the humblest of men he could of course not read, this privilege falling only to noblemen and scribes in those far-off days. But Palini felt a pressing need to look inside nevertheless. He stepped nearer to the fire. Its heat was at first prohibitive, but he pressed on. He would endure a moment on the spit to reach this object, which was well within his grasp. His fingers reached for its leather binding. A Latin word was emblazoned on its spine. It meant nothing to him, but he brought the book down from the shelf. It fell open at the last inscribed page and Palini stood there for a moment, transfixed. A pretty pattern met his eyes, accompanied by strange hieroglyphic symbols which, he guessed, must have been some form of writing. He noticed that the pattern echoed the floor at his feet. He had no name for it, but knew it as the shape most beloved by bees.

Just then there was a great commotion behind him. Letting the book slip onto the floor he turned to see a number of Mendican knights crash through the doors, spilling into the room, scattering snow and mud before them. Their faces were bloody and besmirched, their eyes bulging from their sockets with the exertion and exhilaration of war. Pushing his way through the knights there suddenly appeared Gustav, their king. He had evidently sustained an injury or two. The chain mail of his armour had been pierced and when he spoke, which he did in an attitude of mild hysteria, droplets of blood sprayed from his mouth.

"We will prevail. We Mendicans will win the day. We are the better force. The omens may not be in our favour, but they mean nothing. God is with us. Fear not, brave knights. ...Fear not."

He let out an involuntary sigh and slumped into the throne, first having to right himself when he almost lost his balance. There he sprawled in Ludovico's place, the gesture less an act of divine usurpation, Palini supposed, as one of mortal fragility. The throne was propping him up.

"Where is Ludovico? The coward is somewhere nearby. I know it! Find him!"

The knights were about to move off in all directions when Gustav caught sight of Palini. His eyes widened and he curled his lip in disgust, pointing an accusing finger. Nobody moved.

"You! You're the filthy Szark who killed our man, slashed his throat while he slept. It was you! What are you doing here?"

He answered his own question, eyes blazing in fury.

"But why should I be surprised? Spying for Ludovico. You set this trap. You told him of our plan! Where is he?"

Palini could barely speak, and in all honesty no longer knew where truth began and speculation ended. He raised his arms in a gesture of surrender, but as he did so a sudden sharp pain made him catch his breath. He clutched at his side and his hand became instantly bloody. A dark stain was spreading rapidly across his ragged monk's habit. He must have sustained the wound in the skirmish outside, when he had been knocked to the ground. Evidently he had been too fixated on his mission to notice. He fell to his knees with a resigned and weary sigh.

Just then the mightiest of the knights turned towards him. This brute of a man had hitherto remained in the shadows but now walked forward with a terrible sense of purpose. Palini recognised him immediately as the man who had killed Friar Benjamin, and for all he knew the rest of the brothers.

"Leave him to me, my Lord."

Justice took a pace forward and froze in his tracks, instantly recognising the wretch before him.

Palini had avoided the assassin's eyes, only having had the briefest glimpse of the Mendican who had pursued him to the monastery. But now that they were face to face, he saw through the mass of scar tissue that obscured the lieutenant's features to the purity, the beauty of the face he had known and loved.

Justice was no taller than his father, but twice as broad. For many years he had dreamed of taking revenge against Palini. He had imagined him grovelling at his feet, pleading for his life. But this man half-kneeling, half-squatting in a pool of his own blood was beyond pleading. This man was dying. It would be a mercy to help him on his way. The Mendican drew his sword.

"Luke…?" Palini groaned. "Luke, is that you?"

Palini, poised somewhere between this world and the next, looked up at his son with eyes full of love. The look was not returned.

"I am Justice," whispered the warrior. "That is my name."

Palini seemed not to hear him. When he spoke it was as though his voice came from some other place, from the mountains perhaps, or the deep ocean.

"Luke, my boy … We are together at last."

The bloodstain was spreading thickly across his middle. Palini would indeed be joining Luke very soon, with or without the help of a sword. And the sooner, the better, thought Justice. Behind him, Gustav yelled out from the throne.

"What are you waiting for? Kill him!"

"Tell me," said Palini, in between small gasps, as by now he was struggling to breathe, "what happened to the brothers? What of Friar Benedict, Friar Jacob?"

This brought forth a snarl of contempt. How could Palini sit in judgement? Was he himself not a callous murderer?

Salt tears sprang unbidden to Justice's eyes, tears of self-pity and rage. Perhaps it was the utterance of that blessed word: brother. Even now, in his death throes, Palini could not acknowledge his living son. Justice inwardly cursed himself for his weakness. The sword in his hand ached to find Palini's throat. One flick of the wrist would extinguish this guttering flame. But Palini's words further confounded him. That word leaped out at him once again.

"Tell me of your brother Matthew. Tell me he is alright. You see everything from your seat in Heaven. Find him for me. So many times I thought of him, and wanted him by my side. The night he left I went in pursuit. But I lost the trail. I lost him."

The old man was delirious. Now it was Justice who could barely speak.

"You lost him long before then," he whispered, openly weeping now.

Gustav was becoming impatient. He craned his neck to hear.

"What's happening? Why don't you kill the Szark traitor?"

Palini's smile as he gazed up at him was so sweet and loving that Justice felt his grip on the sword weaken. His father spoke more quickly now, rushing to get the words out, knowing they would be his last.

"I did your brother a great wrong. I punished him for the sin of living in your place. But I was punishing myself."

Justice could no longer contain his emotion. Tears streamed down his face.

"Too late for sentiment. And too late for your other son, the one who was less than perfect."

Palini looked lost.

"But each of you was perfect. That was my mistake. Each of you is perfect, Luke!"

"I am not Luke," bellowed the stricken boy, the lonely boy with the scarred face, "I am MATTHEW!"

"I will kill him myself!" came an equally loud cry from the throne.

Gustav had drawn his sword and was trying to raise himself up, blood now drooling in a steady stream from his lips. His knights rallied to assist him. It was a pitiful sight and the lieutenant, glancing backwards, was suddenly overcome with disgust, not only for Gustav, but also for all that he represented, all the anger of men that he had enjoined, and inspired. Well, as he seemed to have reclaimed his name after all these years, perhaps he could be Matthew after all. Perhaps he might start his life over. He would be Justice one last time. Barely pausing to think, he lifted his sword and whirled it about his head. Turning away from his father slumped beneath him, the Mendican warrior then brought the sword down with a fearsome crash against the wall, shattering it in half but in the process severing the thick rope that held the great iron chandelier in place.

With a great whoosh of air the six-sided contraption hurtled down, giving the Mendican elite below no time to move out of the way. The many candles around the rim were extinguished in the downward plunge, as was the King of Mendica, struck squarely on his crown by the central hub of the hexagonal wheel. No one even cried out, so quickly had the downward plunge done its work. Now the only source of light was the still blazing fire. In its orange glow Matthew could just make out the throne, along with the broken bodies of Gustav and his guards, lying buried under iron staves, thick chains and smoking candles.

---oOo---

It was a time of plenty for the worms who crawled beneath the earth and the buzzards circling above. Between them lay a feast of still warm flesh, and an end to winter's deprivations. Higher in the sky, beyond the clouds, a flock of birds was passing overhead, returning from their winter habitat, as insensible of the human drama being acted out below as the men staring up with sightless eyes were oblivious of their homeward journey.

---oOo---

Matthew looked down upon his father's gaunt body. Was he finally dead, or merely sleeping? For all his sinewy bulk the lieutenant was powerless to resist the waves of love that washed over him, ebbing and flowing so that he was no more substantial in their wake than driftwood on the tide. He saw at last that, had he died at birth and Luke lived, then he, Matthew, would have been the sainted one and Luke the sinner, that in the end only a name had denied him his brother's fate, and only a name had denied Luke his.

All of a sudden Palini gasped once, and slumped back even deeper, seeming to become a part of the castle floor. His hand, which had been clenched, opened and a tiny metal object left it, as his final breath left his body. The object rolled across the hexagon tiles until it came to rest perfectly in the middle of one of them. Justice stared at the coin, barely visible in the half-light of the throne room. The hexagons spread out in all directions. Each six-sided shape was bounded by six of its fellows in an interlocking ring. But while each one was thus surrounded, it was itself part of a ring that surrounded each of the others that surrounded it. 'We are one,' the hexagons seemed to be saying, if only Matthew could decipher this sign from God.

We are all one.

"The day is ours. And we have yet to fire a shot."

The voice was Ludovico's, and it cut across the silence, startling Matthew. He instinctively reached for his sword, but Ludovico was clearly unarmed and posed no threat. He paused and instead used his hand to wipe the tears from his cheeks. How long had Ludovico been standing there? What had he seen? The king spoke calmly, a weary smile playing about his lips.

"I know not who you are, Szark or Mendican, but you have played your part in the victory. We will need men like you, strong men, to help us in the days ahead. If you so wish you may cease your wandering, and come home to Metagoria."

---oOo---

It was dark at the base of the spiral staircase that wound upwards, vanishing into a deeper darkness above. Palini did not know what lay up there, but he knew that he must ascend, and he felt no fear. The steps were worn in their middle from the endless comings and goings, and this further comforted him. Many had been on this journey before. He slowly began to climb around the central column. As he did so the view up ahead remained the same, each rising stone being replaced by another further on, giving him the illusion that he was staying in one spot. He had taken leave of his son, as his wife had taken leave of him, not willingly but happily, since there was nothing to be done. He had said goodbye.

As he ascended, so all the many burdens he had carried throughout his life were lifted from him, one by one, until he felt as light as air. He looked down at his hands in the half-light of the spiral passageway and saw with interest that a mysterious transformation was occurring.

Where before they had been as gaunt and emaciated as his body, now they were soft and unformed, like a child's hands. His monk's habit fit him far more snugly now. It felt warm against his skin. There were no ragged edges or mud spatters. Of the bloodstain that had signalled his demise there was no trace. The pain in his side had gone. It seemed after all that there were miracles, and that everything was magic.

The sense of wonder that gripped Palini was instantaneous and raw, surpassing and obliterating day and night, making nonsense of truth and falsehood, blurring fiction and reality, cowardice and bravery, poverty and riches, innocence and guilt. Heaven and Hell combined and recombined in new and fanciful configurations in his mind. There were no odd or even numbers now. All things were one thing, each dissolving into its opposite. There was no up or down, inside or out, no crying or laughter, no hatred, nor was there even love. This wholeness, this all, this essence, was beyond love.

There existed neither birth nor death.

As Palini reached the top of the staircase there was one last revelation awaiting him. He saw, finally, that man could do God's will neither by humbly accepting whatever crossed his path, nor by forging one of his own, for there was in the end no path to follow, but only this peaceful and heavenly ascent into God's good grace.

Through the shroud of darkness he could just make out the heavy wooden door ahead. He felt for the doorknob, tried to turn it, but found that it was locked. Someone was there, beyond the door, someone he knew he must not meet, though he wanted to. Yes, he wanted to, but the door would not yield. A great weariness came over him. He hesitated for a moment then sat down with his back to the impenetrable barrier.

---oOo---

Had the room not been circular, Dromo would have sat in a corner. As it was, he had shifted his position from seated at the desk to crouched underneath it, then to his present position, using the cell door to rest against. The terrible cries from below had eased, to be replaced by groans of mortal agony. He clamped his hands over his ears to shut out the sound. It proved impossible. The pitiful sadness in those fading, forlorn voices seemed to match and reflect back to him the turmoil within his soul.

Dromo was damned. He had turned his back on the love of God. Already a murderer, he had become a torturer. His beautifully crafted cannons, though silent, stood in readiness to kill his fellow humans. All the evil he had done had been wrought from his need to cling to this sanctuary where now he hid from its consequences. The books that had been his life would now be always out of reach.

Their creator still lived. Well, then, he decided, he would join the battle. He would throw himself unarmed upon the nearest pikestaff, not caring one jot whether it were wielded by friend or foe. This act of self-destruction would be both salvation and punishment rolled into one. He clambered to his feet and pushed against the door, but it would not open. There was someone there, on the other side, someone he knew he must not meet. A great weariness came over him and he sat back down. They were very close now, these two, only the thickness of the door between them.

Seeing he could not exit down the spiral staircase Dromo looked towards the slotted window. It seemed to offer him a way out.

The problem was immediately apparent. The little monk was not so little as he had once been. Even in the olden days, only six moons past but seeming like a lifetime ago, he would have had to wriggle and jiggle his corpulent mid-section through that narrow gap to escape the tower. Of course back then it had never occurred to him to do so. Now, he realised, it was hopeless to even try.

And yet…

And yet he must leave. Somehow he knew that it was time to go, and at the same time that he could take only one route, all other options now denied him. The very cell that had been his home now seemed to be rejecting him, ejecting him. It was as though the walls were collapsing upon him downwards, upwards and inwards, pushing him towards that window. Yes. The room itself was moving, and he was being squeezed now, suffocated. From his position on the floor he brought his knees to his chest. In vain he stared at the pitiless opening that approached, that hopelessly narrow slot in the wall. It was crudely fashioned from blocks of cold, unyielding stone, and he was soft flesh and brittle bone. So many hours, days, weeks he had stared out of it, now it stared back at him. If only he could go through, but it could not be. It could not.

"Why," he thought in despair, "why am I so round?"

---oOo---

Twin boys, as yet nameless, identical in every aspect, lay curled in their mother's womb, separated only by the thinnest membrane, drawing sustenance from her body through their bellies. Her blood was their blood, and they breathed easy in its warming bath. Every hair on each boy's head, every eyelash, every pore had its counterpart,

231

its mirror image in the other. Six moons had been and gone, another three would pass in this heavenly suspension, this angelic liquid state where all was known, before the harsh light of ignorance could steal them away to earth and a new life. All that they knew would be forgotten, but for now all was peace and perfection.

Then the unthinkable happened, in the space of a single heartbeat.

It is impossible for us, in this cruel world of light, to imagine how the two boys knew, upon the instant, that one of them was about to die down there, but know they did. And we may only speculate as to the feelings and emotions that passed between them: fear, perhaps, and certainly regret and longing. They fell to weeping silently. They wept not for the one who was to die, nor for the one who was about to be born, for they cared not which was which. They wept only for one thing: that they were about to be separated, that they could not be together for all time.

---oOo---

Palini woke from the deepest sleep he had ever experienced, feeling more refreshed and alert than he had ever felt. He almost sprang to his feet, realising with pleasure that he felt no stiffness in his legs, and no pain anywhere in his body. He turned the doorknob and pushed gently. This time the door opened onto a circular cell, flooded with sunlight. He was not surprised when he found the cell empty, and he was not disturbed on pushing the door closed to hear a loud click, as of someone turning a key in the lock. Trying the door again he found it had indeed been locked, but far from feeling alarm at being suddenly trapped in this high tower, he felt only relief. No one would disturb him, and there was plenty to occupy his mind.

Looking around, he saw a desk with a quill pen and a supply of ink at the ready. There was a stool next to it, but precious little else in the room. Above his head a pigeon cooed gently, perched on a cross-beam. He thought it the most beautiful creature. Just one feather might describe the universe and everything in it. Next he caught sight of two identical books set in an alcove. These he knew, beyond a shadow of a doubt, belonged to him, to do with as he pleased. He took one down and placed it on the small, wooden desk. With one finger he traced the fine tooling of its ornate leather binding.

Then, out of the corner of his eye, he saw the robe. It was fashioned from the most exquisite purple silk, trimmed with ermine, and it was draped across the sill of the long, narrow window that looked out across the rooftops of Boroglass and the mountains and plains of Metagoria beyond. The wearer of this robe had evidently left through that narrow gap in a hurry. Palini rose on tiptoe and tried to look out of the window. The view did not allow him to look directly down. He hoped the wearer of the robe had not perished. Then he noticed to his surprise that the fields around the castle were empty, where before they had been strewn with warriors, alive and fighting, or dead and lying in bloody heaps. He had evidently been sleeping a very long time because there was not a soul in view, neither Szark nor Mendican, nor even Metagorian. The weather, too, had changed. There was no trace of snow on the ground, and he smiled to see that the thin stem of a plant, snaking its way past the window from where it had rooted in a crevice on the castle wall, somewhere out of sight, was now in bud. He turned back to the book. Its virgin parchment gleamed up at him invitingly. He could neither read nor write, yet it seemed such a trifling thing to learn.

He had all the time in the world.

---oOo---

Dromo emerged from the water, spluttering and gasping for air. He was naked but the sun's rays, emerging from behind a cloud, warmed him. Looking up at the expanse of sky he muttered a prayer of thanks. God in His infinite wisdom had seen fit to place a moat around the castle and it had broken his fall. How strange. Dromo had never realised it was there. Without it he surely would have perished in the fall from the window. He turned his back on the castle and made his way across a field, delighting in the soft caress of the grass beneath his feet, marvelling at the crocuses and wild flowers that were beginning to sprout everywhere. He was heading for the town of Boroglass, where he could see smoke curling up from several chimneys. There would be people there who would clothe him and look after him. He fancied he knew their names.

There would be food. Dromo wanted nothing more than to eat. He wanted fresh bread and olives and cheese. He wanted meat, and fish and broth. The more he thought of food the hungrier he became, and as he quickened his pace his short, stumpy legs seemed to grow longer with every stride.

Six Moons

ACKNOWLEDGEMENTS

On the evening of the 22nd of December 2009 we were sitting in a private room of the Queen Charlotte's Maternity Hospital in Hammersmith, London. Two young doctors were giving us the news in hushed tones: our identical twin boys would not survive. At 26 weeks into the pregnancy they had succumbed to a condition familiar to – and dreaded by – couples in the same boat as us, namely Twin-to-Twin Transfusion Syndrome, TTTS for short. This is where nutrients from the single placenta pass unevenly between the two babies who are joined to it, so that one twin is being starved while the other is being unnaturally force-fed.

The prognosis was as bleak as it could be, and coming only a year after our daughter Iris had been stillborn at 24 weeks, it was devastating. To add to the trauma there was talk of my wife having to deliver the stricken baby boys 'naturally', as we were told a Caesarean might make it harder for her to have healthy babies down the line.

Later still we were sitting alone and in a state of shock when a new doctor, a surgeon, entered the room. He spoke of how we were 'between a rock and a hard place'. Nevertheless, he held out the slimmest of chances: with the aid of keyhole surgery an instrument could be inserted into Hannah's womb with a tiny laser attached. The surgeon would then carry out the enormously tricky procedure of remotely navigating between veins and arteries to carefully slice the placenta in two, literally dividing it between the babies, so halting the fatal transfer of fluids and perhaps giving them a chance of being born alive. No promises were made, for even if they did live they would still have to face the hazards attendant on their severe prematurity.

I will never know how Hannah and I got through the next 24

hours. The procedure was carried out in the morning and it seemed to go well. We asked the friendly Asian doctor his name. He laughed and told it to us, adding, correctly as it turned out, that we were in no fit state to remember names, especially his. We hung on desperately all that day but there was worse in store. In the early hours of the next day another doctor doing routine checks listened to Hannah's tummy for the two heartbeats. He could find only one.

Christmas Eve that year was one of the coldest I remember, but we were scarcely aware of that as our tiny babies came into the world by Caesarean section and were immediately placed in their large, plastic boxes with the tubes and wires attached. Our surviving child, Joseph, had made miraculous progress in a short time and was rushed to the Intensive Care Unit. His twin Rafal, (the name is Polish from his mother's side of the family), identical down to the last hair on his head, was wheeled off to – who knows where? His body was brought to us in a little wicker basket sometime later. He was wrapped in a blanket, looking like a tiny but perfect china doll.

Our boys weighed only a pound and a half each at birth. Joseph was put on a ventilator and didn't leave hospital, still only weighing five pounds, until three months had gone by, after which began the agonisingly long, slow years of his recovery, punctuated by endless trips back to hospital, often in the middle of the night after the latest scare. Joseph was a fighter but had chronic lung disease and a host of other complications resulting from his early arrival. He threw up every meal. For the next four years he barely slept, and of course neither did we.

To be simultaneously blessed and bereaved is a confusing state, especially so given that the babies were identical. We know from day to day how Joseph's brother would have grown, how he would have looked, spoken and moved. For me, and perhaps many others, the experience of having twins gave rise to some very odd philosophical rumination: if we had simply swapped their names would Rafal have lived instead of Joseph? That was a crazy idea born of sleep deprivation, but a far more profound thought gradually dawned: is our superficial difference from each other as unique and separate human beings mere illusion? Over time these conflicting thoughts and feelings found their expression in this strange story.

Ten years on, Joseph is fit and well, a more lovable and eccentric child you could not wish to meet. Whatever hardships we suffered in the early years we have been repaid for them a thousand times over by Joseph's daily presence in our lives. He knows about his lost siblings, cries for them and sometimes speaks to them in Heaven. We had been too distraught in the hospital to remember to ask for someone to take Rafal's picture before he was taken to the mortuary, and have regretted it ever since. However, with the help of Queen Charlotte's friendly administrators I was recently able to track down the name of the surgeon who saved Joseph.

I am happy to have this opportunity to acknowledge our wonderful NHS and those doctors at Queen Charlotte's who gave up their Christmas Eve to save our son's life. And Mister Ruwan Wimalasundera, thank you for proposing that delicate laser surgery, and for carrying it out so skilfully.

Thank you Robbie Fox for your continued love and support.

Special thanks go to my dear friend Mark Thomas for his cover illustration.

But most of all I thank the twins' mother, my wife, who faced all that heartbreak with courage and dignity, and is still doing so.

ABOUT THE AUTHOR

David Richard Fox is a playwright, actor and theatre director whose stage work has been professionally produced in the UK and America. He has written plays for the East End Theatre Group, Red Shift, Pit Prop, Action P.I.E. and Theatre Venture among others. 'Sweet as a Nut', for Art Depot Theatre, was a warped love story based in a shady telemarketing firm that won a prestigious fringe award for Best Comedy in 1990. A children's series for Radio 4, 'Time Hops', co-written with Alan Gilbey, was given a Writers' Guild Award in 1995 and has since been repeated several times. He was lead writer and sometime script consultant on 'The Tribe', Channel 5's apocalyptic teen drama that ran for five years. The show has a cult following around the world. A list of David's many TV credits, more than 150 in total, can be found at **www.davidrichardfox.moonfruit.com.**